"Oops! Excuse me." He turned around.

Now here's someone with a kind face, Marigold thought. Too bad he was a farm lad. It would be a waste of time to talk to him, since he wouldn't have a suit of armor. But she wanted to know what someone who looked so kind would say.

She smiled at him, feeling shy because he looked so nice. "Er, pardon me. What would you do if you won the contest and became prince?"

He liked her dimple. "What?" What had she said? "Sorry."

None of the others had apologized for anything. "That's all right." She repeated the question.

"I don't know." He wished he had a good answer. "I don't want to be a prince."

Ah. What a good answer.

BOOKS BY
Gail Carson Levine

Ella Enchanted
Dave at Night
The Wish
The Two Princesses of Bamarre

THE PRINCESS TALES:

The Fairy's Mistake
The Princess Test
Princess Sonora and the Long Sleep
Cinderellis and the Glass Hill
For Biddle's Sake
The Fairy's Return

The Princess Tales

Volume Two

Cinderellis and the Glass Hill
For Biddle's Sake
The Fairy's Return

Gail Carson Levine

ILLUSTRATED BY
Mark Elliott

HarperTrophy®
An Imprint of HarperCollinsPublishers

Harper Trophy® is a registered trademark of HarperCollins Publishers Inc.

The Princess Tales, Volume II

Cinderellis and the Glass Hill
Text copyright © 2000 by Gail Carson Levine
Illustrations copyright © 2000 by Mark Elliott

For Biddle's Sake
Text copyright © 2002 by Gail Carson Levine
Illustrations copyright © 2002 by Mark Elliott

The Fairy's Return
Text copyright © 2002 by Gail Carson Levine
Illustrations copyright © 2002 by Mark Elliott

Library of Congress Cataloging-in-Publication Data
Levine, Gail Carson.
The princess tales : volume II / Gail Carson Levine ; illustrated by Mark Elliott.—
1st Harper Trophy ed.
    p.   cm.
    Summary: Humorous retellings of a Perrault tale, Andrew Lang's "Puddocky," and the
Grimm Brothers' "The Golden Goose," in one volume.
    Contents: Cinderellis and the glass hill — For Biddle's sake — The fairy's return.
    ISBN 0-06-056043-6
    [1. Fairy tales. 2. Folklore.] I. Elliott, Mark, ill. II. Title.
PZ8.L4793 Pqe 2003   2002068548
398.82—dc21   CIP
                                                                                AC

Typography by Andrea Vandergrift
❖
First Harper Trophy edition, 2003

Visit us on the World Wide Web!
www.harperchildrens.com

CONTENTS

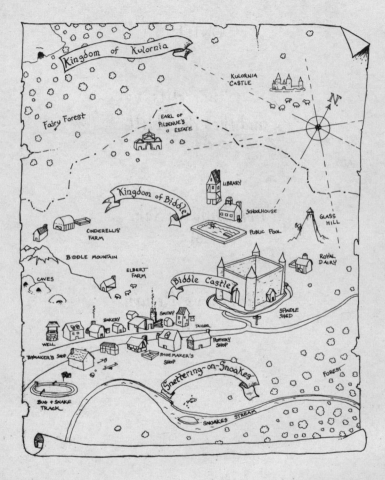

Cinderellis
and the Glass Hill

To Nedda,

zesty, kind, and true—

my dear friend.

—G.C.L.

One

$\mathcal{E}$llis was always lonely.

He lived with his older brothers, Ralph and Burt, on a farm that was across the moat from Biddle Castle. Ralph and Burt were best friends as well as brothers, but they wouldn't let Ellis be a best friend too.

When he was six years old, Ellis invented flying powder. He sprinkled the powder on his tin cup, and the cup began to rise up the chimney. He stuck his head into the fireplace to see how far up it would go. (The fire was out, of course.)

The cup didn't fly straight up. It zoomed from side to side instead, knocking soot and cinders down on Ellis' head.

Ralph and Burt came in from the farm. Ellis ducked out of the fireplace. "I made my cup fly!" he yelled. The cup fell back down the chimney and tumbled out into the parlor. "Look! It just landed."

Ralph didn't even turn his head. He said, "Rain tomorrow."

Burt said, "Barley needs it. You're covered with cinders, Ellis."

Ralph thought that was funny. "That's funny." He laughed. "That's what we should call him—Cinderellis."

Burt guffawed. "You have a new name, Ellis—I mean Cinderellis."

"All right," Cinderellis said. "Watch! I can make my cup fly again." He sprinkled more powder on the cup, and it rose up the chimney again.

Ralph said, "Beans need weeding."

Burt said, "Hay needs cutting."

Cinderellis thought, Maybe they'd be interested if the cup flew straight. What if I grind up my ruler and add it to the powder? That should do it.

But when the cup did fly straight, Ralph and Burt still wouldn't watch.

They weren't interested either when Cinderellis was seven and invented shrinking powder. Or when he was eight and invented growing powder and made his tin cup big enough to drink from again.

They wouldn't even try his warm-slipper powder, which Cinderellis had invented just for them—to keep their feet warm on cold winter nights.

"Don't want it," Ralph said.

"Don't like it," Burt said.

Cinderellis sighed. Being an inventor was great, but it wasn't everything.

⚓ ⚓ ⚓

In Biddle Castle Princess Marigold was lonely too. Her mother, Queen Hermione III, had died when Marigold was two years old. And her father, King Humphrey III, was usually away from home, on a quest for some magical object or wondrous creature. And the castle children were too shy to be friendly.

When Marigold turned seven, King Humphrey III returned from his latest quest. He had been searching for a dog tiny enough to live in a walnut shell. But instead of the dog, he'd found a normal-size kitten and a flea big enough to fill a teacup. He gave the kitten to Marigold and sent the flea to the Royal Museum of Quest Souvenirs.

Marigold loved the kitten. His fur was stripes of honey and orange, and his nose was pink. She named him Apricot and played with him all day in the throne room, throwing a small wooden ball for him to chase. The kitten enjoyed the game and loved this gentle lass who'd rescued him from being cooped up with that disgusting, *hungry* flea.

King Humphrey III watched his daughter play. What an adorable, sweet child she was! Soon she'd be an adorable, sweet maiden, and someone would want to marry her.

The king sat up straighter on his throne. It couldn't be just anyone. The lad would have to be perfect, which didn't necessarily mean rich or handsome. Perfect meant perfect—courageous, determined, a brilliant horseman. In other words, perfect.

When the time was right, he, King Humphrey III, would go on a quest for the lad.

Two

When Cinderellis was old enough to start farming, his brothers gave him the rockiest acres to work, the acres that went halfway up Biddle Mountain, the acres with the caves he loved to explore.

"It's a small section," Burt said, "but you're no farmer, Cinderellis."

"Not like us," Ralph said. He smiled his special smile at Burt, the smile that made Cinderellis ache with longing.

"Do we have any popping corn?" Cinderellis asked, excited. This was his big chance to prove he *was* a farmer. Then Ralph and Burt would smile the special smile at him too.

He took the popping corn and mixed it with flying powder and extra-strength powder. Then he stuffed the mixture under the biggest rocks on his acres. He

"HIS MASTERPIECE WAS THE CARROTS,
RISING LIKE A BALLERINA FROM A TINY
TINY TIP."

added twigs and lit them.

The corn popped extra high. The rocks burst out of the ground and rolled to the bottom of the mountain. The soil became light and soft and ready for planting. Cinderellis mixed his seeds with growing powder and planted them. Then he set up an invention workshop in his biggest cave.

At harvesttime Cinderellis couldn't wait for his brothers to see his vegetables. His carrots were sweeter than maple syrup. His tomatoes were redder than red paint. And his potatoes were so beautiful, you could hardly look at them. Ralph and Burt would have to admit he was a farmer.

Cinderellis sprinkled balancing powder on his vegetables and loaded them on his wheelbarrow. Then he pushed the wheelbarrow to the barn without losing even a single ruby red radish.

Ralph and Burt were still in the fields, so Cinderellis arranged his vegetables outside the barn door. Using more balancing powder and a pinch of extra-strength powder, he stacked the tomatoes in the shape of a giant tomato and the beets in the shape of a giant beet. His masterpiece was the carrots, rising like a ballerina from a tiny tiny tip.

Finally his brothers drove up in the wagon behind Thelma the mule.

Burt took one look and said, "Tomatoes are too red."

Ralph tasted a carrot and said, "Carrots are too sweet."

Burt added, "Potatoes are too pretty."

Cinderellis said, "But carrots should taste sweet, and tomatoes are supposed to be red." He shouted, "And what's wrong with pretty potatoes?"

Ralph said, "Guess I'll load them on the wagon anyway."

Burt said, "Might as well take them to market."

Cinderellis left them there. He went to his workshop and screamed.

⚓ ⚓ ⚓

When Marigold was seven and a half, King Humphrey III left Biddle Castle again, to go on a quest for water from the well of youth and happiness. Marigold missed him terribly. She told Apricot how miserable she was. Apricot purred happily. He loved it when his dear lass talked to him, and he was sure it meant she was in a good mood.

Marigold patted the cat. Apricot was wonderful, but she wished for a human friend, someone who would understand her feelings, someone who would rather be home with her than be anywhere else in the world.

❧ ❧ ❧

It was the end of the first day of fall, and Cinderellis was nine years old. He woke up exactly at midnight because his bed had begun to shake. On the bureau the jars of his wake-up powder and no-smell-hose powder jiggled and rattled.

But as soon as he got up to see what was going on, the shaking stopped. So he went back to sleep.

In the morning Ralph and Burt and Cinderellis discovered that the grass in their best hay field had vanished.

A tear trickled down Ralph's cheek. "Goblins did it," he said.

Burt nodded, wiping his eyes.

Cinderellis walked across the brown field. Huh! he

thought. Look at that! Hoofprints! He picked up a golden hair. "It was a horse with a golden mane," he announced. "Not goblins."

His brothers didn't listen. Ralph knelt and poured dirt from his left hand into his right. Burt poured dirt from his right hand into his left. Cinderellis got down on his knees too. Although he didn't see what good it would do, he poured dirt from his left hand into his right. Then he poured it from his right hand into his left.

Ralph said, "Get up, Cinderellis. Don't be such a copycat."

Cinderellis stood, feeling silly. And lonelier than ever.

Three

$\mathcal{D}$uring the winter after the hay disappeared, King Humphrey III returned. He hadn't found the well of youth and happiness, but he'd brought home a flask of coconut milk that was supposed to be just as good.

The milk didn't make anyone a day younger or a smile happier, though. All it did was make people's toenails grow, a foot an hour. This kept the Chief Royal Manicurist busy for a week, till the effects wore off.

Marigold waited for her turn with the manicurist in the throne room with her father and all the nobles who'd had a sip of the milk. Everyone's boots and hose were off, and the smell made Apricot sneeze on his cushion next to Marigold's chair.

Marigold didn't mind the smell. She was too happy about seeing her father to mind anything—until he mentioned that he was planning a new quest, this time for a pair of seven-league boots.

Marigold would have left the room, if she had been able to walk with three-foot-long toenails. As it was, everybody saw her cry.

⚓ ⚓ ⚓

A year to the day after the hay vanished, Cinderellis' farmhouse shook again in the middle of the night. In the morning the hay was gone again from the same field, and Cinderellis picked up another horse hair, a copper one.

Every night for the next year, Ralph practiced a spell to scare away the goblins.

Goblins, go away *NOW*!
Go go go go *GO*!
Away away away away *AWAY*!
Now now now now *NOW*!

"The words are hard to remember," Ralph said.
Burt agreed. "Almost impossible."
Even though he knew that goblins had nothing to do with the disappearing hay, Cinderellis wanted to help. So he invented goblin-stay-away powder. It was

made of dried vinegar and the claw of a dead eagle, the two things goblins fear most.

The first day of fall came. At night Ralph headed for the barn, which was right behind the hay field. He'd wait there for the goblins and say the spell.

"Let me come along," Cinderellis said. "I'll bring my goblin-stay-away powder."

"Don't need you," Ralph said. He smiled his special smile at Burt.

Burt smiled back. "What good would you be?" he asked.

In the middle of the night Cinderellis was still awake, because he was having imaginary conversations with his brothers, conversations in which they were amazed at how wonderful his inventions were. Conversations in which they begged him to be their friend.

At midnight the ground shook. Cinderellis smiled. Now Ralph would see that he, Cinderellis, had been right all along. Now Ralph would see the horse.

The next morning Ralph was already eating his oatmeal when Burt and Cinderellis sat down for breakfast.

"Hay all right?" Burt asked.

Ralph shook his head. "Rain today."

"Have to get the corn in," Burt said. "What happened?"

"Ground shook. Said the spell. Went to sleep. Hay was gone."

"Did you see the horse?" Cinderellis asked.

"What horse?"

"Didn't you look outside the barn?"

Ralph smiled at Burt. "What for?"

Burt guffawed.

Later that day Cinderellis found a silver horse's hair in the hay field.

The following year it was Burt's turn to spend the night in the barn. In the morning the hay was gone.

"My turn next," Cinderellis said, picking up a golden horse hair from the bare field.

Ralph and Burt roared with laughter.

"My turn next," Cinderellis insisted, turning red. He'd save the hay. His brothers would admire him at last. And he'd never be lonely again.

⚓ ⚓ ⚓

A month after Burt's night in the barn, King Humphrey III returned to Biddle without finding seven-league boots. What he had found were three shoes that walked backward, very slowly. They went straight to the Royal Museum of Quest Souvenirs.

Marigold asked her father when he would go off on his next quest. He said he was leaving in three days to find the lark whose song is sweeter than harp music.

Marigold nodded sadly and went to her bedchamber, where she patted Apricot's head and thought gloomy thoughts. Apricot closed his eyes, glad that his dear lass was happy.

Cats are so loyal, Marigold thought, swallowing her tears. They never go off on quests. They never leave you alone and lonely.

Four

Cinderellis spent day after day in his workshop cave, getting ready for the horse's arrival. He needed something to keep it from grazing, so he invented horse treats. They were made of oats and molasses and a few other ingredients to make the treats particularly scrumptious to horses—ground horse chestnuts, minced horse mackerel, and chopped horse nettles.

And since horses are partial to apples, Cinderellis made the treats apple shaped. He tried them out on Thelma and she liked them, even though she was a mule. Horses would adore them.

After he'd perfected the treats, Cinderellis turned one of his caves into a stable—an unusual stable, where the water trough refilled itself from a rain barrel outside the cave, where the rock floor had been softened by fluffy powder, and where there were paintings of subjects that horses like. Cinderellis had done the paintings himself. One was a close-up of three blades of spring grass. Another was of the ground as it would look to a galloping horse. And the last was of trees as they'd look to a cantering horse.

It was a lot of effort for just one night—because after that Ralph and Burt would probably keep the horse in the barn with Thelma. But Cinderellis didn't mind. It would be worth everything if he could be friends with his brothers. A little extra work didn't matter compared to that.

⚓ ⚓ ⚓

In the middle of the summer King Humphrey III returned from his quest. But instead of the lark that sings more sweetly than a harp, he brought home a mule whose bray drowns out an orchestra.

A week later, the king left on a quest for the goose that lays golden eggs.

Marigold noticed that the other castle children were laughing at the latest quest souvenir. Whenever she and Apricot approached a group of them, they'd be braying as hard as they could. When they saw her, they'd run away, giggling.

Marigold wished she could be a part of their group and laugh along with them. The king's souvenirs *were* funny. They would make her laugh too, if she had someone to laugh with.

⚓ ⚓ ⚓

Late at night after the first day of fall, Cinderellis snuck out to the barn with a bucket of horse treats. A little before midnight he heard distant hoof-beats. He opened the barn door a crack. The grass was still there.

The hoofbeats grew louder. The floorboards hummed. The hoofbeats grew even louder. The rafters hummed along with the floorboards. Cinderellis' hands shook and his teeth rattled.

Then the shaking stopped. A copper-colored mare stepped into the field. She was the biggest, most beautiful horse Cinderellis had ever seen. Across her back lay a knight in copper armor.

This was a surprise. Cinderellis hadn't expected anyone to be on the horse.

"SHE WAS THE BIGGEST, MOST BEAUTIFUL
HORSE CINDERELLIS HAD EVER SEEN. ACROSS
HER BACK LAY A KNIGHT IN COPPER ARMOR."

The mare lowered her head and started to graze.

She mustn't do that! Cinderellis thought. He grabbed the bucket of horse treats and left the barn.

The horse looked up and saw an ordinary farm lad, but she liked his face. He could rescue her from the evil magician who had put a spell on her and her two sisters. The lad only had to touch her bridle and she'd be safe. The spell would be broken, and she wouldn't have to return to the magician ever again. She let the lad come right up to her. Touch the bridle, she thought. Touch the bridle.

He held out the horse treats.

She sniffed the bucket. Mmm, pleasant. She put her head in the bucket and started to munch. Yum, delectable. And the treats were shaped like apples. Great combination!

Take the bridle, lad. Please!

Cinderellis grabbed the bridle. I've got you now, he thought.

Aah! The mare was so happy. She loved this lad. She would do anything for him.

Cinderellis put the bucket down and tiptoed to the knight lying across the mare's back. "Sir, are you all right?"

The knight didn't move.

"Sir?" Cinderellis raised his voice. "Sir? Can you hear me?"

The knight didn't answer.

Cinderellis tapped the metal. "Excuse me, sir. I hope you don't mind . . ."

Nothing.

He tapped louder. It sounded hollow. He lifted the couter, which covered the knight's elbow. It felt too light. If an arm were in there, it would be heavier. The knight was just an empty suit of armor! And he'd been talking to it!

Five

Cinderellis led the mare to the stable cave. Inside, he lifted the armor off his back and dumped it behind a mound of hay. He took her saddle and bridle off too. Then he began to brush her.

It felt sooo good. She whinnied softly.

What should he call her? He wanted a name that meant something.

He had it. Chasam. It stood for Copper Horse Arrives Shortly After Midnight. He picked up a handful of oats and fed it to her. "Good night, Chasam."

In the morning Cinderellis led his brothers to the hay field.

"See," he said. "I saved it."

Burt said, "Goblin spell worked after all." He smiled the special smile at Ralph.

It wasn't the spell!

Ralph smiled back. He said, "Just took a while."

"It wasn't the spell," Cinderellis hollered. "I did it!"

"Time to gather the hay," Ralph said.

Cinderellis opened his mouth to tell them about Chasam and then shut it again. What if he told them and they still wouldn't admit he'd done anything? What if they said a goblin had run away because of the spell, but his horse had stayed? That was probably what they would say! And once they saw Chasam, they'd keep her for themselves. They'd never let him have a turn riding her or plowing with her.

Well, he wasn't telling them. Chasam would be his secret. He'd let them have next year's horse—*if* they admitted that he had saved the field. He'd let them have all the horses if they'd be his friends. After all, friends don't hold out on each other.

To get his mind off his brothers, Cinderellis spent the day with Chasam. He rode her, which was nothing like riding Thelma the mule, or even like riding the horses at the yearly fair in Snettering-on-Snoakes. Those horses weren't as tall as Chasam was. So tall you were higher than anybody and felt more important too. And their gaits weren't silken like hers. She hardly jiggled, even when she trotted. And her gallop was completely thrilling. The trees whizzed by, and the breeze that had ruffled Cinderellis' hair when he started out—that breeze was miles behind. Why, he almost caught up to yesterday's thunderstorm.

After an hour Cinderellis dismounted and started tossing horse treats to Chasam. He'd throw them, and she'd run after them and gobble them up. Sometimes she'd catch them before they landed. As time went on she became better and better, till she could catch almost anything he could throw.

It was fun, but he couldn't spend every minute playing, so he stopped and got busy. His drying powder wasn't quite right, and there had been a lot of rain lately. His lettuces were drowning.

He let Chasam graze while he did his experiments. He added ingredients that kept out water—ground umbrella, diced hood of a poncho, and pulverized roof shingle.

Chasam came over and watched.

At least someone's interested in me and my inventions, Cinderellis thought. Even if it's only a horse.

⚓ ⚓ ⚓

Two days before Marigold's thirteenth birthday King Humphrey III returned from his latest quest, bringing with him the turkey that lays tin eggs.

A week later the king mounted his horse in the castle courtyard. He was leaving again, this time to search for the lamp that commands a genie. Marigold begged him not to go.

King Humphrey III reached down and stroked her forehead. "But sweetheart," he said, "wouldn't you like a genie who would make all your wishes come true?"

Apricot squirmed in Marigold's arms. That horse's head was bigger than his whole body. He wanted his dear lass to step away from the horse.

Marigold shrugged. Sure she'd like a genie, so she could wish for her father to stop going on quests. But if he'd just stop on his own, whe wouldn't need a genie. Besides, the king would never actually bring back a genie, so what was the point of wanting one?

Six

Late at night, a year after Chasam's arrival, Cinderellis and the mare waited in the hay field. Cinderellis had a pail of horse treats with him. At a few minutes before midnight Chasam started neighing and running in circles.

At midnight the ground began to tremble. Cinderellis' hands shook. The earth shimmied and lurched. Cinderellis' teeth rattled. The trees swayed and twisted. The hay field churned and pitched. Cinderellis' stomach sloshed.

Then everything grew quiet. A silver mare stepped into the hay field. A suit of silver armor lay across her back. Cinderellis felt disloyal thinking it, but the silver horse was even more beautiful than Chasam. Bigger, stronger, and just a little prettier around her eyes.

Chasam galloped to the mare. They nuzzled. They raced together across the field. They reared up and batted each other playfully with their front hooves. Then, at last, they trotted to Cinderellis and stood by him, their sides heaving.

Cinderellis grabbed the silver mare's bridle. The silver mare was overjoyed. She loved this farm lad and would do anything for him.

"Welcome, Shasam," Cinderellis said. Shasam stood for Silver Horse Arrives Shortly After Midnight. He led her to the stable cave. Inside, he lifted off her armor and tossed it on top of the copper armor.

In the morning Cinderellis showed Ralph and Burt that the hay field was all right.

Ralph said, "Goblins didn't come back."

Burt said, "Good year for turnips." He put his arm across Ralph's shoulder. They walked to the barn, leaving Cinderellis standing by himself.

He swallowed the lump in his throat. He wasn't going to give Shasam to his brothers either.

She was even more fun to ride than Chasam. Faster, smoother, *mightier*. She was better at catching horse treats too. But Cinderellis didn't want to hurt Chasam's feelings, so he pretended he never noticed the difference.

⚓ ⚓ ⚓

The following June King Humphrey III returned home. Instead of finding the lamp that commands a genie, he had stumbled over the candle that rouses an imp. The imp was so angry about being bothered that he put a curse on the king—King Humphrey III had to go home and stay there. No quests for five whole years.

The king was heartbroken. His next quest was going to be the most important one ever. Marigold was old enough to get married, and he'd planned to find the perfect lad for her. And now he couldn't.

Marigold was sorry her father was unhappy, but she was delighted that he was going to stay home. She was also delighted that he couldn't search for her husband. It would be awful to have to marry something he brought back from a quest.

Apricot noticed the king weeping, and he worried that his dear lass might be sad too.

The day after he returned, King Humphrey III sat in the throne room and tried to listen to his Royal Councillors, but he couldn't concentrate. Without a quest, how was he going to find the right husband for his darling daughter?

Then he had a brilliant thought. If he couldn't go searching for the right lad, he'd make lots of lads come to him! But how would he know which one was perfect? Hmm. He began to have an idea.

⚓ ⚓ ⚓

Exactly a year after Shasam's arrival, Chasam, Shasam, and Cinderellis waited in the hay meadow for Ghasam (Golden Horse Arrives Shortly After Midnight).

Half an hour before midnight, the wind picked up. Cinderellis felt a tremor. And another. The wind howled.

Midnight came. The ground rocked and bucked. The wind went wild, blowing from every direction. A tree was uprooted and sailed away into the east. Cinderellis' hands shook, his teeth rattled, and his stomach sloshed.

The world went black. The moon had gone out! The stars had gone out! Cinderellis' heart bounced up and down.

Then the wind stopped. The ground steadied. The moon and stars reappeared.

A golden horse stepped into the hay field. A suit of golden armor lay across her back. Cinderellis gasped. She was gorgeous. You looked at her, and you heard trumpets playing and cymbals crashing.

Chasam and Shasam nickered. They cantered to their sister and nuzzled her. Then all three galloped joyously around the hay field, legs flying, necks stretched out, their manes and tails streaming.

Finally they stopped, and Ghasam trotted to Cinderellis. She whinnied as he took her bridle. She loved this farm lad already. She'd do anything for him.

The next morning Cinderellis told Burt and Ralph that the hay would never disappear again. He held his breath and waited. If they thanked him and smiled the special smile at him, then they could have Ghasam.

Ralph said, "Wet weather coming."

Burt said, "Maybe some hail."

Cinderellis breathed out. Nothing had changed. So he'd keep the horses, and he'd have three loyal and true animal friends. Who needed human friends anyway?

Seven

Ghasam was better than her sisters at catching horse treats. And she was faster than they were too. Once, when Cinderellis jumped on her back, he started to sneeze. "A—" he said. She took off. He finished the sneeze. "Choo!" They had gone two miles.

When they got back to the stable cave after that gallop, Cinderellis told Ghasam what a phenomenal horse she was. Then he told Chasam and Shasam what phenomenal horses they were, because he didn't want them to feel left out. He knew only too well what that was like.

⚓ ⚓ ⚓

Princess Marigold turned fifteen. There were banquets and balls and puppet shows in her honor. Everyone said she was the sweetest, kindest, least uppity princess in the world. And pretty to boot.

Nobody mentioned that she was also the most ter-rified princess, because she had told only Apricot about that, and he had misunderstood anyway.

She was scared because of her father and his—well, his crazy ideas. Since he couldn't go on a quest, he had devised a contest to find her future husband. He hadn't revealed the contest rules yet, but he had said that the winner would be courageous, determined, and a fine horseman. Considering the king's quest souvenirs, though, Marigold thought she'd probably wind up marrying a mean stubborn gnome who could ride kangaroos!

The final banquet was almost over when King Humphrey III stood and beamed at his guests. "Dear friends," he began. "Tomorrow our Royal Glass-workers will begin to create a giant hill in the shape of a pyramid. It will be made entirely of glass. When it is completed, our darling daughter will wait at the top with a basket of golden apples. The brave lad who rides his horse up to her and takes three apples will have her hand in marriage."

Marigold fainted. Her father was too excited to

notice. Except for Apricot, nobody noticed. They were too astonished. Apricot was worried. Had his dear lass eaten something that disagreed with her?

King Humphrey III continued. "We will also give the provinces of Skiddle, Luddle, and Buffle to the winner to rule immediately. And he will be king of all of Biddle after I'm gone. Any lad can compete. All he needs is a horse and a suit of armor."

After she recovered from her faint, Marigold tried to persuade her father to change his mind. But he wouldn't listen. He said the winner of the contest would be perfect for her and perfect for Biddle.

Marigold disagreed. The man who won the contest would be cruel and evil. No kind person would make a horse climb a glass hill.

And she would have to marry him.

⚓ ⚓ ⚓

In a week the pyramid was built. Its glass was clearer than a drop of dew and slipperier than the sides of an ice cube. King Humphrey III wasn't completely satisfied, though, because it was level on top. But Marigold had flatly refused to sit on a point.

37

The pyramid's actual point was made by a cloth canopy that would be over the princess's head, giving her shade. King Humphrey III sighed. It would have to do.

The king announced the contest in a proclamation. Cinderellis heard about it from Ralph at breakfast. Not because Ralph told him. No. Ralph told Burt. Naturally.

"The contest starts tomorrow." Ralph laughed. "Burt, do you think Thelma wants to climb a glass hill?"

Burt laughed for five minutes straight. "That's funny," he said.

Ralph said, "Want to see it?"

Burt said, "Wouldn't miss it."

They didn't ask me if I want to see it with them, Cinderellis thought. Well, he didn't. He wanted to climb the pyramid. He wondered how slippery the glass was.

Cinderellis didn't want to become a prince and marry a princess he'd never even met. He just wanted to see if his sticky powder would take him and one of the mares up the glass hill. And then he wanted to show the golden apples to Ralph and Burt. They were giving up a day of farming to see the contest. That meant they cared about it. And they'd love the golden apples. They were farmers, after all. They loved fruit. When Cinderellis gave the apples to them, they'd love him too.

He took some sticky powder from his room and started walking toward Biddle Castle.

⚓ ⚓ ⚓

Dressed as a Royal Dairymaid, Princess Marigold wandered through the field around the pyramid. She passed gaily colored tents and neighing, stamping horses and shouting, striding knights and squires. There are hundreds of contestants, she thought. And not one of them had even asked to meet her. All they wanted was to rule Skiddle, Luddle, and Buffle. And to make their poor horses go up a stupid glass hill.

But perhaps there was one man among them who would be a good ruler, even if he didn't care about her. Maybe he had an extraordinary horse who didn't mind trying to climb glass, a horse so well treated that it would do anything for its rider.

If such a man was here, she had to find him and figure out how to get him to the top.

She squared her shoulders. To find him, she had to talk to all of them, all the horse torturers. That was why she had dressed as a Royal Dairymaid and left Apricot in the castle—so no one would suspect she was a princess.

⚓ ⚓ ⚓

Cinderellis saw the glass hill from a mile and a half away, sparkling in the sunlight. It was as high and almost as steep as the castle's highest tower. When he got close, he saw the Royal Guards surrounding the pyramid. He knew one of them—Farley, who used to sell candy apples at the yearly fair in Snettering-on-Snoakes.

Cinderellis asked Farley to let him touch the glass hill. Farley looked around to make sure nobody was watching. Then he nodded.

Cinderellis barely felt the hill because his hand slipped off so fast. For a second it felt lovely—cool and smoother than smooth. And then his hand was back at his side. He tried again. Mmm, pleasant. Whoops!

"A lot of people are here, aren't they?" Cinderellis said.

Farley turned to look at the crowd. Quickly, Cinderellis tossed a handful of sticky powder on the hill.

"Yup," Farley said.

Three quarters of the powder rolled off the hill! If sticky powder, which stuck to *everything*, rolled off, then that hill was the slipperiest thing Cinderellis had ever seen, felt, or imagined.

Eight

Princess Marigold hadn't talked to a single contestant who would be a good ruler. Some wanted to
raise taxes. Some wanted to have hunting parties all
the time. One even said he'd declare war and take
over all of Biddle! Another said he'd drown Apricot,
because he didn't want cat hair all over everything!
If either of them reached the top of the hill, she'd
kick him all the way to the bottom. She'd *swallow*
the golden apples before she'd let either of them get
his hands on them.

After talking to at least a hundred contestants,
Marigold gave up. She just stared at the pyramid,
trying not to bawl.

Cinderellis stared at it too. He imagined climbing
it while Ralph and Burt watched.

He said good-bye to Farley and backed into a person

behind him. "Oops! Excuse me." He turned around.

He'd bumped into a Royal Dairymaid. A pretty one, with a sweet face, a very sweet face.

Now here's someone with a kind face, Marigold thought. Too bad he was a farm lad. It would be a waste of time to talk to him, since he wouldn't have a suit of armor. But she wanted to know what someone who looked so kind would say.

She smiled at him, feeling shy because he looked so nice. "Er, pardon me. What would you do if you won the contest and became prince of Skiddle and Luddle and Buffle?"

He liked her dimple. "What?" What had she said? "Sorry."

None of the others had apologized for anything. "That's all right." She repeated the question.

"I don't know." He wished he had a good answer. "I don't want to be a prince."

Ah. What a good answer. "But if you had to be?"

He wondered why she wanted to know. But why not? He was curious about lots of things too. "I guess if I were prince, I'd create inventions that would make my subjects' lives easier." That's right. That's what

"'I DON'T KNOW.' HE WISHED HE HAD A GOOD
ANSWER. 'I DON'T WANT TO BE A PRINCE.'"

he *would* do. What could he invent for a Royal Dairymaid? "For example, I'd invent cow treats." He nodded, figuring it out. He'd leave out the special horse ingredients and add some ground cow parsnip and dried cow shark instead. "The cows would love the treats, and they'd love to be milked."

"That would be a great invention," the princess said. He wanted to do something that animals would like! This lad would never torture a horse.

Nobody had ever encouraged Cinderellis before. She was the nicest maiden in Biddle. "I already invented horse treats," he said, boasting a little.

"They must be delicious," Marigold said. Gosh! she thought, he's already done something to make horses happy. "Um," she added, "if you did become a prince, would you go on quests?"

Cinderellis shook his head. "When I want something, I invent it, or invent a way to get it." He added in a rush, "Most of my inventions are powders that do things." He stopped. "You're probably not interested."

"I am! Please tell me about them." If she knew him better, they might be friends—her first human friend.

"Well, my first invention was flying powder." He

told her about the powders.

She listened and asked questions. Cinderellis had never had so much fun in his life. This Royal Dairymaid was splendid!

Marigold had never had so much fun either. She especially liked the idea of fluffy powder. You'd always have a soft place to sit, and—oh my! "Your fluffy powder could save lives. If a person—or, say, a cat—fell out of a window, you could sprinkle fluffy powder on the ground. And the cat wouldn't be hurt." She beamed at him.

He beamed back. "I'm thinking of using my sticky powder—"

"Oh no!" Marigold saw the king heading their way. "I'd better go. I have some milking to do." She curtsied and fled into the crowd.

"Where do you . . . When could I . . ."

But she was gone, and he didn't even know her name.

Nine

Back in his workshop cave, Cinderellis got to work. Sticky powder alone wouldn't get him up the glass hill, so he mixed in extra-strength powder and a few other ingredients. While he invented, he thought about the Royal Dairymaid. He wished he'd had a chance to tell her he was going to climb the pyramid. Then she could have watched and rooted for him.

But she might have thought he wanted to marry the princess. He didn't. He wanted— He stopped mixing. He wanted to marry the Royal Dairymaid! He hadn't felt lonely for a second while they'd talked.

But he didn't know her name, so how could he marry her? Well, she was a Royal Dairymaid, so he should be able to find her again. There couldn't be that many of them.

Suppose he didn't show the golden apples to Ralph

and Burt. They might like the apples, but they probably wouldn't be interested in his special sticky powder, since they never cared about his inventions, not one bit. So suppose he hid the apples instead, till the princess married somebody else. Then suppose he sold them and used the money to set up an invention workshop in Snettering-on-Snoakes. He'd do what he'd said a prince should do—invent things to make people's lives easier. He'd sell his inventions, and he'd marry the Royal Dairymaid.

He started mixing again. Yes, he'd marry her. That is, if she'd have him.

The powder was ready to try out. He spread it on Ghasam's front hoof.

She couldn't lift her foot. She strained. Finally she forced it up—with grass and dirt attached.

Too strong. He cleaned off her hoof. Then he added a pinch of this and a teaspoon of that and spread the mixture on Shasam's hooves.

Now the powder didn't work at all. Shasam could even gallop. He frowned. Maybe his on-off powder was in the "off" phase when her feet were on the ground and in the "on" phase when her feet were in

"THE POWDER WAS READY TO TRY OUT."

the air. That would mean that the sticky powder was only active when there was nothing to stick to.

He could fix that. He tapped each hoof with a stick. That should reset the phases.

There. Each step was difficult, and Shasam had to strain a little to lift her hooves, but she could lift them and the grass and dirt didn't come up too. Good.

Now he needed to add his time-release powder, which would turn the stickiness on when they started climbing the glass hill and turn it off when they got back to the bottom.

⚓ ⚓ ⚓

Marigold woke up in the middle of the night. She had dreamed of a secret weapon that would keep a horse and rider from getting to the top of the glass hill. With her secret weapon she wouldn't have to marry someone who was mean and nasty and cruel. She patted Apricot, who was curled up next to her, and fell back to sleep, smiling.

Early the next morning Royal Servants climbed a ladder to the top of the pyramid. They brought with them an outdoor throne, a picnic lunch for a princess and a cat, the basket of golden apples, and a water bowl for Apricot. When they came down, Marigold carried Apricot and the secret weapon to the top. As soon as she got there, the Royal Servants took the ladder away and the contest began.

⚓ ⚓ ⚓

After breakfast the same morning, Ralph said, "Good day to watch a glass hill." He guffawed.

Burt guffawed.

Ralph pushed back his chair and walked out of the farmhouse. Burt pushed back his chair and followed him. Cinderellis wondered if the Royal Dairymaid would be watching the contest.

At the workshop cave, he worked on his powder some more. Finally he thought it was ready.

⚓ ⚓ ⚓

At first Marigold had been ready with her secret weapon whenever a horse galloped at the pyramid. But rider after rider failed to climb up even one inch, so she relaxed and became interested in looking down on everything. The knights and squires seemed no bigger than her hand, and their cries and the neighing of their horses sounded muffled and thin.

Only Biddle Mountain appeared as big as ever, looming in the distance, much higher than the glass hill.

The day grew warmer and Marigold grew hot—hot and bored. Apricot was hot too, but he knew his dear lass had brought him up there to show everyone how important he was to her. So he rubbed himself against her leg and purred.

Marigold wished she knew the name of the nice farm lad. Even if she never saw him again, though, she'd remember their conversation forever.

⚓ ⚓ ⚓

Cinderellis wanted to scream. He'd been putting the copper suit of armor on for hours. He'd finally gotten the tasset and the mail skirt on over his waist and hips. The cuisses and the poleyns and the greaves were on his legs. The sabatons were on his feet. The vambraces were on his arms. The couters were over his elbows.

But the breastplate kept popping off!

Over and over he'd hammered it here and bent it there. And it would hold—for about ten seconds. Then—*POP!*

At this rate he'd never get to the pyramid.

Ten

A knight on a black stallion prepared to climb the hill. The stallion looked bigger than any of the other horses. Marigold reached for her secret weapon.

But the stallion's hooves slipped off the pyramid as soon as they touched it. The knight made the horse try again—and the horse slipped again. The knight wanted to try a third time, but everybody yelled that he should let the rest of them take a turn.

Burt and Ralph laughed so hard, their sides hurt.

Marigold put her secret weapon down and started breathing again. It was three thirty. Only a few more hours till it would be too dark to see the hill and she could come down. Only a few more hours and it would be over forever.

But then her father would come up with another horrible plan.

⚓ ⚓ ⚓

Cinderellis had finally wedged the breastplate under the fauld. And he'd managed to mount Chasam, even though it had taken over an hour. He'd picked Chasam because she'd looked so disappointed when he'd tried the powder out on Ghasam.

He pulled the gauntlets over his hands. Now for the helmet. Uh-oh. He couldn't make his hands in the gauntlets do anything. He'd never get the helmet on. He took the gauntlets off again and put the helmet on.

Now he couldn't see to put on the gauntlets. He could only see through one chink in the visor, just enough to steer Chasam.

Well, he didn't need to see. He could feel. There. The gauntlets were on.

Now where were the reins? He couldn't tell through the gauntlets. Were these the reins? He hoped so.

He kicked Chasam, harder than he meant to. She didn't mind. They were off. It was five o'clock.

⚓ ⚓ ⚓

Two more horses to go. Marigold scratched under her tiara. She felt hot and sticky. Apricot was drinking from his water bowl. She was glad he was up here with her. She wished that kind farm lad were here too. She'd introduce him to Apricot, and he'd invent something nice for a cat.

One more horse to go.

Marigold wondered what her father would dream up next. Maybe he'd make her sit at the bottom of a glass hole, and the horse that didn't crash down and squash her would have her hand and Skiddle, Luddle, and Buffle.

The last horse, like the 213 before it, failed to climb the hill. Marigold stood up. At last. She hadn't needed her secret weapon. Wait! What was that? A cloud of dust coming from Biddle Mountain?

In the field below, King Humphrey III couldn't see the dust cloud. He decided that the contestants could all try again tomorrow. He didn't want to end the contest after just one day when it was so important.

Then he heard people shouting. There was another rider? Let him come, then. Maybe this one would be enough of a horseman to climb the pyramid. Maybe this one deserved Marigold.

Cinderellis saw the pyramid through the chink in the visor. They were almost there.

Everyone was astonished at the beauty and size of the copper-colored mare. Everyone was also amazed that such a glorious horse would let herself be ridden by that nutty knight or whatever he was. For one thing, his armor was tarnished and filthy. His posture was terrible. His hands and the reins were flopping around in his lap. He wasn't even really riding the mare. She was carrying him, like cargo.

Marigold's heart started pounding.

Chasam cantered up to the glass hill. Cinderellis sort of kicked her to keep going. She placed her front right hoof on the hill. She leaned her weight on it. It held!

She started to climb. The watching crowd grew silent.

Marigold didn't know what to do. If this mare climbed the hill, it would be because she wanted to. Any fool could see the mare's rider wasn't making her do anything. But the rider still could be mean and nasty. Marigold picked up her secret weapon.

But maybe he's nice, she thought, as nice as the farm lad. She had to find out. At least she had to see his face. "Sir!" she called. "Please take off your helmet."

Who was yelling? Cinderellis could see only the glass hill in front of him. He tried to look up, but all he saw was the inside of the helmet. Was something wrong? He tried to push his visor up. Nothing happened.

"I'd like to see your face," Marigold called.

Somebody was yelling again. Cinderellis decided to take the helmet completely off. He pushed up on it. Nothing happened.

Chasam was a tenth of the way up the hill. The crowd on the ground almost stopped breathing.

He's trying to do what I want, Marigold thought. That's something. And he didn't force the horse up the hill. She laughed. If he couldn't even get his helmet off, he'd never be able to pick up the apples—if he climbed all the way up.

She thought of tossing the apples into his lap. If nobody ever got to the top, the next contest could be worse than this one. Or her father might let this contest go on forever, and she'd spend the rest of her life up here.

She put the secret weapon down. The apples were next to the throne. She took one, aimed carefully, and threw. The apple landed on Chasam's saddle, in the

57

little valley between the saddle and Cinderellis' mail skirt.

Huh! Cinderellis thought. Did something hit me?

Marigold picked up another apple. She would have thrown it, but she got worried. She was taking an awful chance. She hadn't seen the knight and she hadn't talked to him. Maybe they could talk, even if she couldn't see him. "Sir," she called, "what would you do if you ruled Skiddle, Luddle, and Buffle?"

"What?" Cinderellis yelled. "What? Speak louder."

A roar came from the helmet. Marigold didn't hear words, just a roar. Whatever was in the armor didn't know how to talk. It could only roar. It was a monster! And she'd given it an apple!

Eleven

Marigold reached for the pitcher that held her secret weapon. But she hesitated. She didn't want to hurt the horse.

Chasam was a third of the way up the hill. And climbing.

The monster would be up here in a minute. She had to do something! She'd try to use only enough to make the mare slide down slowly. She leaned over the edge of her platform and poured a thin stream of olive oil down toward Cinderellis.

Everyone watching wondered why the princess was leaning over the edge of the pyramid. They were too far away to see the pitcher of oil.

The powder wasn't made to withstand olive oil. Chasam started to slip.

Cinderellis thought, We're going down! Is Chasam

hurt? What went wrong with the powder?

Chasam couldn't drop Cinderellis. She loved him too much. She spread her legs so she wouldn't topple over and slid down slowly.

Ralph's and Burt's mouths dropped open. What a mare! Any other horse would have fallen on its head, or on top of its rider.

At the bottom of the pyramid Chasam turned around and took off at a gallop.

⚓ ⚓ ⚓

King Humphrey III issued a proclamation announcing that there would be a second and a third chance to climb the glass hill.

⚓ ⚓ ⚓

Cinderellis lay panting in the dirt in front of the workshop cave. Chasam, Ghasam, and Shasam were grazing nearby.

It had taken him a half hour to get his helmet off. Once it was off, he'd used his teeth to tear the gauntlets off his hands. And then he'd squirmed out of everything else.

His powder had failed. He had failed.

Shasam sniffed the golden apple, which had fallen into the parsley patch. Cinderellis picked it up, and Shasam cantered a little ways off, ready for a game of horse-treat catch. But Cinderellis was too depressed for games. Besides, Shasam might break a tooth on the stupid golden apple.

One apple wouldn't buy a workshop in Snettering-on-Snoakes. He wouldn't be able to marry the Royal Dairymaid on just one apple. He might as well not have it.

Still, he wondered how he'd gotten it. The only explanation he could think of was that the princess had thrown it to him. But why would she?

He stood up and carried the armor and the apple into the cave. He dumped the armor on the heap with the other armor and hid the apple behind an outcropping of rock. Then he headed to the farmhouse for dinner.

Ralph and Burt were just finishing up.

"Did anyone win the contest?" Cinderellis asked.

"Not today," Ralph said. He smiled his special smile at Burt.

Cinderellis didn't even notice.

"Maybe tomorrow," Burt said.

Tomorrow?

"Or the day after," Ralph said.

He had two more chances!

"There was a beautiful mare," Ralph added.

"Mare's rider was an idiot," Burt said.

"Real idiot," Ralph said.

They both laughed.

"Work to do," Cinderellis said. He ran out of the farmhouse. He had to find out what had gone wrong with his powder. And then he had to fix it.

He'd marry that Royal Dairymaid yet!

In the stable cave he lit a lantern and bent over Chasam's left front hoof. She whinnied and blew warm air across his forehead.

Hmm. The hoof looked greasy. Cinderellis touched the greasy spot. He tasted it.

Olive oil! They'd used olive oil to make the pyramid slipperier. How could they do that without telling? It wasn't fair.

What would repel olive oil? Drying powder might help, but drying powder worked best on water. Olive pits mixed with drying powder? Olive pits were surrounded by olive oil right there in the olive, and they never became soggy, so they must repel the oil. Yes, that should do it. He ran to the farmhouse pantry for olives and olive oil.

⚓ ⚓ ⚓

In the morning Marigold asked the Chief Royal Cook to refill her secret weapon pitcher. But the Chief Royal Cook was fresh out of olive oil. Marigold said walnut oil would be fine.

In the field around the glass hill the contestants prepared for the day's trial. A knight painted sticky honey on his horse's hooves. A squire scraped his stallion's shoes to make them rough. Another knight screwed hooks into his mare's shoes.

Outside the workshop cave Cinderellis poured olive oil down a rock that was about as steep as the glass hill. Then he dusted his new powder on Ghasam's hoofs. She started to climb and then slipped. Cinderellis added a little more olive-pit powder and told Ghasam to try again.

⚓ ⚓ ⚓

The knight who had painted honey on his horse's hooves galloped up to the glass hill. His horse tried to step onto the hill but slipped right off.

Marigold petted Apricot. It was going to be another long, hot day.

Ralph grinned at Burt. Burt grinned at Ralph. It was going to be another fun day.

⚓ ⚓ ⚓

It had taken all morning and almost all afternoon, but Cinderellis' new powder was ready. And Cinderellis was ready, in the silver armor. It had been easier to get into, because he'd learned a few tricks the day before. But being inside was as bad as ever. He could hardly see anything, and his hands were almost useless inside the gauntlets. Still, he was in it, and he was mounted on Shasam. Chasam had earned a rest. He'd ride Ghasam tomorrow if anything went wrong today.

But what could go wrong?

Twelve

The sun was setting behind Biddle Mountain. I didn't need the oil at all today, Marigold thought. But then she saw a dust cloud in the distance. Oh no! Could the mare be coming back? Could the monster be coming back?

People started yelling. "The mare! The mare!"

But it wasn't the copper mare. This horse was a mare, but she was silver and even bigger than the copper mare. One thing was the same, though: The same fool was riding as yesterday. Anyone could see that, even though the rider wore dirty banged-up silver armor instead of dirty banged-up copper armor.

Cinderellis and Shasam reached the pyramid. Shasam started to climb the hill. It wasn't hard. She began to trot.

Marigold was terrified. The mare was halfway up the hill. Where was the walnut oil? She put Apricot down and reached for it. The hem of her gown knocked into the basket that held the apples and sent an apple clattering down the pyramid.

Shasam saw the apple. *Horse treat!* She veered and caught it with her teeth. Then she started climbing again.

Marigold poured the walnut oil. Shasam was two thirds of the way up the glass hill, but when the oil touched her hooves, she started to slip. Oh nooo! She fought, and her hooves beat the glass.

At first Cinderellis thought Shasam was dancing. But no, she was falling. Was she all right? Was she hurt?

Shasam slid down the same way Chasam had. At the bottom she made sure Cinderellis was still in the saddle. Then she galloped away, still holding the golden apple between her teeth.

⚓ ⚓ ⚓

Cinderellis was furious. How could they have switched oils on him?

And what would they use tomorrow?

And how had Shasam gotten a golden apple? He couldn't even guess, and he didn't have time to think about it anyway. He had to figure out how to fix his powder. What he needed was an all-purpose oil repellent. On the farm they grew the nuts and grains for every kind of oil that Biddlers used. What if he ground up the hulls and pits of all of them and added that to the powder? It was a big job, but when he was done, he'd have an all-purpose oil-repellent extra-strength time-release on-off sticky powder that would climb any glass hill anywhere.

Inventing the new powder took all night and most of the next day, but finally it was ready. Cinderellis started putting on the golden armor. It was too big, so he dusted it with shrinking powder. And made it too small. So he dusted it with growing powder. And made it too big. He wasn't used to working in such a rush, and he hated it. He sprinkled on just a little shrinking powder. And made it exactly the way it had been when he started. He was going to bounce around in it, but it would have to do. When the contest was over, he was going to invent better armor.

⚓ ⚓ ⚓

Marigold waited for the dust cloud. Everybody else was waiting too.

And there it was—the dust cloud.

The mare was golden this time, and so splendid she took Marigold's breath away. Why did such a marvelous horse let a monster ride her?

Cinderellis ached all over from crashing into a different part of the armor whenever Ghasam took a step. Not only that, his helmet kept bouncing around too. Sometimes he could see outside pretty well. Sometimes he could just see a little. And sometimes all he could see was the inside of the helmet. Whenever he could see, he pointed Ghasam toward the pyramid and hoped for the best.

They reached the glass hill. Ghasam started climbing. Cinderellis' helmet shifted. All he could see now was gray metal and three rivets.

Marigold didn't waste a second. She went right for her pitcher of oil, which was walnut again. She leaned over the edge of the pyramid and started pouring.

The oil flowed down the hill. It reached the mare, but it didn't stop her. She didn't slip a bit. She just kept climbing.

Marigold dropped the pitcher and picked Apricot up. She petted the cat and trembled. She was going to have to marry the monster.

Cinderellis felt Ghasam climb higher and higher. It's working! he thought. If only he could see.

Ghasam stepped onto the platform and stopped. She didn't like being so high up. She shifted from foot to foot.

Cinderellis wondered why Ghasam had stopped. Were they at the top? Had they made it? He tried to move the helmet so he could see. He banged on it, but it didn't budge. He tried to raise the visor, but it wouldn't budge either. How would he get the third apple if he couldn't see?

Marigold hugged Apricot even tighter. Too tight, the cat thought. He wished that she'd stop squeezing and that the horse would go away.

Marigold screamed, "Stay away from us! I won't marry you!"

Somebody was yelling again. "What?" Cinderellis yelled back.

That sounds like a word, Marigold thought. But what was it? What difference did it make? She yelled, "Go away! Leave us alone!"

"What?"

She got it! It had said, "Cat." It wanted Apricot! The monster wanted Apricot! "I'll never give him up, not even if you torture me."

Ghasam wished her dear lad would tell her what to do. She took a step back and then a step forward. She hated it up here.

"What? What is it? What's happening?" Cinderellis shouted. If only he could see. If only he could hear. If only he could find the apple.

Marigold made out another word. The monster had said "cat" again, and "apple." It was saying she better give it the apple or it would take the cat! She jumped up and down with fear and anger. "You can't have them! Go away!"

Cinderellis shoved at the visor and banged the helmet. *Ping!* It sounded like a rivet popping out, but the visor still wouldn't budge.

Ghasam wanted to go home. She took two steps forward.

It's coming at me! Aaaaa! It's going to get us! It can have the apple. Marigold rushed to the basket and snatched up an apple. Then she darted forward and placed it on the saddle in front of Cinderellis.

Apricot hated being so near a horse. He hissed and shot out a paw.

Ghasam shied back. Cinderellis bounced in the saddle. His helmet snapped back, and he stared at the inside of it where his nose should have been. The visor came off and fell onto the platform, but the visor opening was over his forehead, way above his eyes.

Ghasam shied again. Cinderellis' legs knocked into her sides. He wanted her to leave. At last. She started down the hill. At the bottom she began to gallop.

On top of the pyramid Marigold picked up the golden visor. The monster had gone at last.

But it had three apples.

Thirteen

Every day Cinderellis walked to Biddle Castle. He asked all the Royal Dairymaids about his Royal Dairymaid. Nobody knew her. The Royal Dairymaids swore there was no such person.

What good was it to have the golden apples without his sweet, adorable Royal Dairymaid? No good at all.

⚓ ⚓ ⚓

King Humphrey III waited a week for someone to show up with the golden apples. When no one did, he and his Royal Pages went from house to house, looking for the lad whose armor matched the golden visor.

Marigold came along. She wanted to be there when they found the monster so she could do something.

She didn't know what, but something. She left Apricot home to keep him safe for as long as possible.

Two weeks after the last day of the contest, the king reached Cinderellis' farm.

Ralph was weeding the alfalfa field.

King Humphrey III didn't think the fellow looked brave or determined or at all like son-in-law material, but he asked anyway. "Did you climb the glass hill? And do you have a suit of golden armor and three of the princess' golden apples?" He gestured at Marigold.

Ralph bowed to the king. "Nope."

Burt said the same exact thing when they found him in the barley field.

"Are you two the only ones on the farm?" Marigold asked.

"Yup." Then he remembered. "I mean, nope. We have another brother, Cinderellis, but he didn't go to the contest."

"Where is he?" King Humphrey III asked. Burt pointed to Biddle Mountain.

Cinderellis was outside his workshop cave, inventing armor improvements, when Ghasam whinnied. He turned and saw the king and his attendants heading up the mountain.

Cinderellis picked up the pieces of armor and ran into the cave, shooing the horses in ahead of him. Then he rushed to his tomato patch and started weeding.

The king reached the tomatoes. Cinderellis stood and bowed. Then he stared. The Royal Dairymaid was with him. His heart started racing. What was she doing here?

It was the nice farm lad! Marigold smiled in delight.

Cinderellis wondered why there were jewels on her gown.

"Did you climb the glass hill?" King Humphrey III asked. "And do you have a suit of golden armor and three of the princess' golden apples?" He gestured at Marigold.

She was the princess? "Yes! Yes! I have them! I'll get them!" He ran into the workshop cave.

Marigold thought, He's the monster? How could he be?

Cinderellis came out of the cave, leading Chasam, Shasam, and Ghasam. In his arms were the golden helmet and the three golden apples. He put everything down and knelt before Marigold. "Will you marry me?"

He was smiling up at her. He still looked nice. But then why had he wanted Apricot? "Why did you try to take Apricot?"

What was she talking about? "What apricot?"

"My Apricot. My cat. I had him with me on top of the glass hill."

Cinderellis started laughing. He put on the helmet, jamming it hard over his head. The visor space was over his forehead again. "I can't see anything," he said.

Marigold laughed too. He sounded like the monster. "Take off the helmet," she said.

She was saying something, but he couldn't hear what it was. Did she say she'd marry him? He pushed up on the helmet. It wouldn't come off. "It's stuck."

"Yes, I'll marry you."

What did she say?

"DID SHE SAY SHE'D MARRY HIM? HE PUSHED
UP ON THE HELMET. IT WOULDN'T COME OFF.
'IT'S STUCK.'"

Epilogue

In three days Cinderellis and Marigold were married.

Ralph and Burt came to the ceremony. As soon as it was over, they smiled their special smile at each other and hurried home to harvest the corn.

Chasam, Shasam, and Glasam became Marigold's pets, just as Apricot was. The only difference was that the horses couldn't fit on the princess' lap. Apricot got used to the horses and even became friends with them. He liked Cinderellis too, once he was convinced—after a few misunderstandings—that his dear lass was happy with the lad. And he loved Cinderellis' first invention as crown prince: cat treats.

Marigold loved all Cinderellis' inventions. She and Cinderellis celebrated their wedding anniversary every year with a demonstration of his all-purpose sticky powder on the glass hill, which they kept polished just for the purpose.

King Humphrey III resumed his questing when the imp's curse ended. He returned with so many souvenirs that an extra wing had to be added to the Museum of Quest Souvenirs.

Cinderellis never went on a single quest. His only trips were to Skiddle, Luddle, and Buffle, and Marigold always went along. While there, she made so many friends that she was never lonely again.

Cinderellis' wetting powder cured a drought in Skiddle, and his drying powder worked wonders on the floods of Buffle. What's more, he showed the Luddlites how to use growing powder on their wheat crop. Everyone was so grateful that Cinderellis became the most popular ruler in Biddle history. He was never lonely again either.

And they all lived happily ever after.

The End.

For
Biddle's
Sake

All my love to Rani and Ronnie—

friend, fellow artist, sister.

—G.C.L.

One

When she was two years old, Patsy tasted a sprig of parsley at a traveling fair. She loved it, and from that moment on, the only food she would eat was parsley. After a while her parents, Nelly and Zeke, began to call her that, Parsley.

The trouble was that parsley grew in only one spot in the village of Snettering-on-Snoakes, and that spot was the garden of the fairy Bombina, who was renowned for turning people into toads.

Nelly said she couldn't let her daughter starve, and Zeke, who rarely spoke, nodded.

So every Thursday night, Zeke would head for Rosella Lane, where he'd climb the high wall that surrounded the fairy's garden. He'd stuff a sack full of fresh parsley and return home. His stealing went undetected for three years because Bombina was serving time in the dungeon of Anura, the fairy queen. Bombina's crime was failure to get along with humans.

Meanwhile, Parsley grew into a plump, happy child with a lovely smile, in spite of teeth that were stained a pale green.

Then Bombina returned.

That Thursday evening, she strolled in her garden and saw Zeke gathering armloads of parsley. Armloads! She would have turned him into a toad on the spot, but she had already reached Anura's legal limit of five human-to-toad transformations per fairy per year, and she didn't want to go back to jail.

"What are you doing?" she shrieked.

Zeke grabbed the parsley and ran. Bombina stood on her left foot and blinked twice. Zeke froze, unable to move a muscle. Bombina thought of turning him to stone, but stone wasn't her specialty. Her specialty was toads.

"Why are you stealing my parsley?" she thundered. Then she unfroze Zeke's mouth.

Zeke wasn't used to talking. So even though his mouth could move, it didn't.

Bombina dropped her voice to a sugary whisper. "I can turn you into a chicken . . ." She never ran out of legal chicken transformations. "A clucking—"

Zeke found his voice. "It's for m-my d-daughter."

His daughter? Anura always said that fairies should be kind to children. Fairies who were kind were her favorites. Bombina was on probation, and she was definitely not one of the fairy queen's favorites.

"Bring your daughter to me."

"B-but—"

"*Bring your daughter to me!*" Bombina unfroze all of Zeke.

He stumbled once, then started to run.

"*And drop the parsley.*"

Back in their cottage Zeke told Nelly what Bombina had commanded. Nelly began to run around frantically, bumping into Zeke and shouting that she wasn't bringing her precious daughter to anybody. Zeke ran around frantically too, and he bumped into Nelly when she wasn't bumping into him.

Bombina materialized in the cottage, right next to Parsley's bed. "Is this your daughter?"

Parsley awoke and sat up, blinking in the bright light

that flashed around Bombina's big pink wings.

"Hello, child," Bombina boomed.

Parsley was frightened. She'd never seen anyone so enormous or so grumpy-looking.

"What's your name, honey?"

Parsley said, "Parsley," in a small voice.

"*Parsley!*" Bombina whirled on Nelly and Zeke. "You dared to name your daughter after my parsley?"

Nelly held her ground. "We named her P-Patsy, Your G-Graciousness, but—"

"Silence!" Bombina leaned over the bed. "Why do you like parsley so much, Parsley?"

Parsley didn't know why. She just did. She stared at Bombina and didn't say anything.

"Answer the nice fairy," Nelly said. "Tell her why . . ."

She's a fairy? Parsley thought. She'd been taught that fairies were gentle and good. Then this one was only pretending to be mean. She smiled up at Bombina.

Nothing was sweeter than Parsley's smile.

A tiny corner of Bombina's heart melted. "Harrumph." She cleared her throat. And had a brilliant idea. Anura would be delighted! "I will take the child home to live with me. Then Parsley can eat parsley whenever she likes."

Live with a fairy! Parsley was thrilled. Maybe she'd learn magic. "Can I, Mama?"

A tear trickled down Nelly's cheek.

A tear trickled down Zeke's cheek.

"Well?" Bombina yelled. "Can she?"

Nelly and Zeke couldn't refuse a fairy. Nelly said, "Yes, Parsley gumdrop, you can go."

Two

Nearby in Biddle Castle, Prince Tansy was in the throne room with his brothers, Prince Randolph and Prince Rudolph, who were arguing as usual. Randolph and Rudolph were twins, and they were nine years old, two years older than Tansy. No one else was in the room.

Tansy could tell the twins apart because Randolph's left nostril was slightly larger than his right nostril, and Rudolph's right nostril was slightly larger than his left.

"The right hand, fool!" Randolph held King Humphrey IV's gilded wooden scepter just beyond Rudolph's reach. "A king holds the scepter in his right hand."

"The left hand, numskull!" Rudolph twisted Randolph's nose and tried to grab the scepter.

With his free hand Randolph twisted Rudolph's nose.

Tansy removed Rudolph's fingers from Randolph's nose and Randolph's fingers from Rudolph's nose. He said, "I think—"

"You don't have to think," Randolph said, trying to grab some part of Rudolph again.

"You'll never be king, Tansy," Rudolph said, lunging for the scepter and getting one hand on it.

Randolph tried to yank the scepter away from Rudolph.

Rudolph hung on and tried to yank it away from Randolph.

Tansy said, "Stop! You'll break it."

Crack! The scepter broke in half.

Randolph and Rudolph dropped their halves and ran out of the throne room. Tansy ran too, although he knew what was going to happen next. The Royal Guards were going to find the three of them. Randolph and Rudolph were going to tell King Humphrey IV that he, Tansy, had broken the scepter, and King Humphrey IV was going to believe them, no matter what Tansy said. Then the king was going to make him write *I will never again break a Royal Scepter* at least a hundred times.

While Tansy ran, he thought about the question his brothers had been arguing over. The solution was simple. A king should hold his scepter in his right hand on Sundays, Tuesdays, and Fridays, and in the left on Mondays, Thursdays, and Saturdays. That would show how fair he was. He should hold it with both hands on Wednesdays. That would show how stable his kingdom was.

Randolph and Rudolph hadn't thought the matter through. They never did.

But one of them would be king anyway, and Tansy never would be, even though he had hundreds of great ideas about how to rule the kingdom of Biddle. Youngest sons didn't become king.

⚓ ⚓ ⚓

Bombina liked having Parsley live with her. She especially liked having Parsley's smile live with her. She'd do anything to see that smile, and anything included some surprising things—smiling back at Parsley or occasionally smiling first, tucking Parsley in at night, and even letting Parsley touch her wings. Bombina had never let anyone do that before.

For her part, Parsley loved living in the fairy's palace, although she missed Nelly and Zeke. Bombina's cook knew dozens of parsley recipes. Parsley could have her parsley scrambled, steamed, stewed, barbecued, braised, broiled, fried, or liquefied. She could have parsley pesto, parsley pasta, parsley pizza, parsley pilaf, or parsley in puff pastry. And for dessert she could have parsley pie, parsley pudding, parsley penuche, parsley taffy, parsley upside-down cake, or, the one she liked best, parsley ice cream sundae with hot parsley sauce and parsley sprinkles on top.

But most of all Parsley loved watching Bombina make magic.

The fairy never used a wand. She began all her magic by standing on her left foot. To disappear, she'd make her chin jut forward and put her left pinky finger in her mouth. And *poof!* she'd be gone. To sink into the ground, she'd bend at the waist and hop twice. A hole would appear, and she'd slide into it till only her head showed.

But the magic that Bombina did most often was

to turn objects into toads. The fairy queen's limit applied only to humans—Bombina could transform as many of anything else as she liked.

Parsley was astonished at the things Bombina turned into toads—a single thread in a bodice, an egg, a tile roof, a picture frame, an umbrella handle.

Once, when her footman Stanley failed to open the carriage door quickly enough, Bombina turned his bushy red beard into a purple Fury-Faced Trudy Toad. It looked funny, hanging upside down from Stanley's chin. Bombina laughed, and Parsley would have too if Stanley hadn't looked utterly shocked.

Parsley tried to cast spells too. For example, she'd let her hot parsley tea cool. Then she'd stand on her left foot, lick her index fingers, and grunt *ung huh tuh* exactly as Bombina would. But her tea never warmed up. She couldn't fly either, or make her slippers come to her from halfway across the bedchamber.

She never tried to turn anything into a toad. It didn't seem right. Maybe Stanley's beard was pleased to be a toad, but maybe it wasn't. Maybe it didn't like croaking and catching flies.

Once Parsley asked Bombina, "Why can't I make

"BOMBINA TURNED HIS BUSHY RED BEARD
INTO A PURPLE FURY-FACED TRUDY TOAD."

magic? It looks simple when you do it." She smiled.

As usual, Bombina was enchanted by the smile. That's another kind of magic, she thought, to be able to smile so charmingly with teeth as green as a green onion.

"You have to be magical to make magic, dear. I'm a magical creature, and you aren't."

Three

Parsley had been living with Bombina for ten months when June 23, Midsummer's Eve, the fairies' New Year, came around. As always, Bombina attended the ball at Anura's palace, where she received, along with the other fairies, her new allotment of legal transformations.

During the ball Bombina told the fairy queen about adopting Parsley. Anura clapped her hands in joy. "Hurrah, Bombina! With your little Oregano you will—"

"Parsley," Bombina said.

"Ah, yes. You will usher in a golden age in your Snetting-Snooks. You and your Tarragon will—"

"Snettering-on-Snoakes. Parsley."

"Whatever. A river of love will flow from humans to you and from you to them. You won't want to turn a single one, not even the most aggravating, into a toad." Anura embraced Bombina and bathed her face in kisses.

When Parsley went into Bombina's bedroom the next morning, Bombina sat up instantly. She couldn't wait to begin her new life of deep and abiding friendship with humans.

"Come here, child." And she kissed Parsley on the forehead.

Parsley didn't know about the fairies' New Year or what Anura had said, but she liked the kiss. She smiled and said, "How are you going to wear your hair today?" She thought Bombina's hairstyling magic was the best magic of all.

"We'll see." Bombina knew Parsley liked to watch, so she decided to try out a few new styles until the serving maid brought breakfast. She sat at her dressing table. Parsley came and stood next to her.

Bombina shook out her long red hair. Then she lifted her right foot, stuck out her front teeth, and said *arr arr arr*. Her hair shrank into her scalp until only a couple of inches were left, and those inches curled into ringlets. She knocked her fists together, and her hair turned blue with blond stripes.

Parsley giggled.

Bombina's stomach rumbled. She frowned. Where was that lazy serving maid?

Ah, well, Bombina thought. Perhaps Cook was preparing something special to please her. Bombina stuck out her chin and said *raa raa raa*. Her hair grew long again and piled itself on top of her head.

"Oooh!" Parsley said.

Bombina's stomach rumbled again. She didn't want something special. She wanted her ordinary breakfast at its ordinary time. But it was too late for that. I must calm myself, she thought. Perhaps the serving maid was carrying my breakfast to me when she fell and broke both her ankles. That would be nice.

Bombina stood up and started to pace.

Uh-oh! Parsley thought. She got out of the way and stood in the window alcove.

Bombina paced and thought. Perhaps Cook fell into the porridge and drowned. That would be nice too.

In fact, the serving maid had quit the night before. The servants knew that the fairies' New Year always brought new toad transformations. Bombina had been kinder lately, but they were still frightened. The year before Bombina had gone to jail, she had turned three gardeners, a manservant, and a seamstress into toads.

No one wanted to deliver Bombina's breakfast. After arguing for a half hour, the servants ganged up on the scullery wench, who had started her job only the week before. Cook carried the breakfast tray to Bombina's door, and two menservants carried the wench. When they got there, Cook put the tray into the scullery wench's hands. One manservant opened the door, and the other shoved her inside.

"There you are!" Bombina shouted while shifting her weight onto her left foot. Then she began to stare at the scullery wench. She lowered her chin to her chest and continued to stare.

Oh, no! Parsley thought. She's going to—

Bombina flapped her right wing once while singing *oople toople* in a high scratchy voice.

The scullery wench looked startled. Parsley heard the beginning of a yelp. The breakfast tray clattered to the floor, and the scullery wench shrank. For a moment she stood there, an orange scullery wench two inches tall. Then she was a toad, an orange Christopher Inquisitive Toad.

Parsley wanted to scream, but she couldn't, or she might be turned into a toad too. She slipped behind the window drapes and peeked through them.

Bombina hiccuped twice, and the toad vanished. She noticed the smashed breakfast tray on the tile floor. Her yummy coddled eggs were a yellow puddle, and her lovely porridge with figs and raisins was hardening into a big brown lump.

She was so angry, she stamped her feet and shrieked *aargh* and accidentally turned a candlestick into a feathered bonnet. Then she stormed out of her bed chamber.

A minute later Parsley crept out too, gladder than ever before to still have two human legs and two human hands and no warts.

Within a quarter hour Cook was a mauve Sir Melvin Dancing Toad, the two menservants were both turquoise Belladonna Spinning Toads, and the laundress, who happened to be in the kitchen, was an ultramarine Ethelinda Bumbling Toad. Bombina had beaten her own record for using up toad transformations.

Four

Parsley felt terrible about the toads. She had liked all of them when they were human, and she had especially liked Cook. Parsley was almost certain that toads ate their food raw, and Cook would hate that.

Bombina did everything she could think of to cheer Parsley up and get her smiling again. The fairy found a new cook who knew a hundred parsley recipes, including one for parsley bubble gum.

Parsley blew big green bubbles, but she wouldn't smile.

Bombina invented fifteen new hairdos, but Parsley still wouldn't smile.

Bombina gave Parsley a magic spyglass that could see anything anywhere in Biddle, no matter what was in the way.

But Parsley still wouldn't smile.

Bombina was frantic. She begged Parsley to smile. She shouted. She wept.

But Parsley still wouldn't smile.

Finally, in desperation, Bombina said, "I won't turn people into toads anymore."

Parsley smiled.

Bombina was so happy that she hugged Parsley with both arms and both wings. But while she hugged, she thought, By next New Year, Parsley will have forgotten my promise.

Parsley loved her magic spyglass. She looked through it at Zeke and Nelly and the new baby. She looked over all of Biddle. She saw Elroy the shepherd's great-great-grandson herd sheep. She saw Ralph's and Burt's grandchildren do their farm chores, and once she even saw Ralph and Burt themselves, sitting on their porch, rocking back and forth, perfectly in time with each other.

Parsley watched the Royal Banquets in Biddle Castle, examining the plates for parsley dishes. She watched the Royal Balls, searching for ladies' hairdos that Bombina could try out. Once she saw a hair ornament atop an especially tall hairdo—a miniature sailing ship, with all sails billowing.

The first time Parsley saw the Royal Family was at a banquet. King Humphrey IV was bald, and his ears stuck out. The twins, Prince Randolph and Prince Rudolph, would have been handsome if they had ever stopped glaring at each other. The youngest prince, Prince Tansy, had freckles, a cowlick, and a serious expression. Parsley thought he looked exactly the way a prince should.

One twin sat on the king's right and the other sat on his left, and they glared at each other around King Humphrey IV's belly. Tansy sat farther down the banquet table, between two Royal Councillors.

The twin on King Humphrey IV's left cut his baked potato the long way, but the twin on the right cut his potato the short way. The twin on the left ate in this order: roast hart, potato, lentils, watercress. The twin on the right ate in the reverse order.

All Tansy was eating was the watercress. Parsley was thrilled. He loved watercress and she loved parsley. They had something in common!

Actually, they didn't. Tansy never ate more than one dish at any meal, so he could give it his undivided attention. The watercress was pretty good, but he didn't love it.

The next time Parsley observed Tansy, he was in the Royal Wardrobe Room with his two brothers. The twins were both trying on King Humphrey IV's red satin Royal Ceremonial Robe. One twin had his arm in the left sleeve and the other had his arm in the right sleeve. Each was struggling to pull the robe away from the other.

They were caroming from one side of the room to the other—smashing into the shelves that held the king's breeches, corsets, codpieces, garters, jerkins, and undershirts. Tansy was dodging the flying Royal Wardrobe and saying something.

Oh no! The Royal Ceremonial Robe was ripping, up from the filigreed hem all the way to the ermine collar.

Now the twins were pulling off the robe and running out of the Royal Wardrobe Room, with Tansy right behind them. Parsley followed him in her spyglass. He dashed through the castle, out a first-floor window, along a cobblestone path, and into the Royal Museum of Quest Souvenirs, where he threw

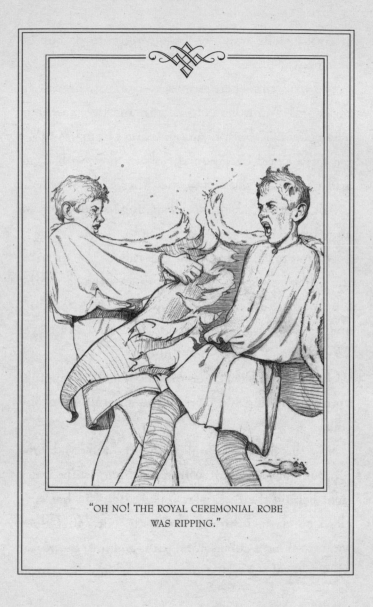

"OH NO! THE ROYAL CEREMONIAL ROBE
WAS RIPPING."

himself into the pile of straw under the turkey that lays tin eggs.

He wormed his way in so far that only the tippy toe of one boot stuck out, and Parsley feared he wouldn't get enough air to breathe.

She turned her spyglass back to the castle, where a search was in progress. A Royal Guard found one twin hiding under a bed in a Royal Bedchamber. Another guard found the other twin under a bed in a different Royal Bedchamber.

Randolph and Rudolph don't have much imagination, Parsley thought, feeling proud of Tansy for hiding in such a good spot. She watched the Royal Guards search Biddle Castle from the cellar to the towers. Then she joined Bombina for lunch.

After lunch Parsley watched the Royal Guards search the Royal Stable, the Royal Dairy, and Queen Sonora's old spindle shed. They searched the museum last and finally found Tansy, who emerged covered with straw and bits of tin. He looked sad and scared. Parsley's heart went out to him.

The Royal Guards marched him to the throne room, where his brothers and King Humphrey IV were waiting. Randolph and Rudolph pointed at Tansy. Parsley saw their mouths shape the words *Tansy did it. He ripped the Royal Robe.*

But he didn't! Parsley thought. He didn't do anything.

King Humphrey IV yanked Tansy up by his ear and shook him. Then he dragged Tansy out of the throne room. Randolph and Rudolph watched him go. They were both grinning.

Royal Rats! Parsley thought.

With the spyglass she followed Tansy and King Humphrey IV along the Royal First Floor Corridor, up the Royal West Tower Stairway, up, up, up to a room at the top of the tower, where there were a desk and a chair and ink and parchment and a quill pen and nothing else. King Humphrey IV left Tansy there, and the prince sat at the desk and began to write.

Parsley focused her spyglass on the parchment and saw—

I will never again rip the Royal Robe.
I will never again rip the Royal Robe.
I will never again rip the Royal Robe.

I will never again rip the Royal Robe.
I will never again rip the Royal Robe.

A tear fell on the parchment and blurred three lines of *never again*. Parsley felt like crying too.

Five

By the time Parsley was fifteen, she had watched Randolph and Rudolph get Tansy in trouble for scores of things he hadn't done—denting the Royal Armor, laming the Royal Steed, breaking the hand off the marble statue of King Humphrey I, and releasing the flea big enough to fill a teacup from the Royal Museum of Quest Souvenirs.

The flea was the worst. It bit King Humphrey IV, and his cheek swelled as big as a teakettle. Tansy spent a whole week in the Royal West Tower that time.

Parsley despised Randolph and Rudolph. She half wanted Tansy to punch each of them in their Royal Noses, but she admired him no end for his forbearance. Whenever she saw him in the spyglass, she smiled and smiled.

One day, Bombina saw her smiling and was

instantly jealous. "What's so special out there?" she roared.

"Nothing," Parsley said nervously. "Just the roses in Biddle Castle's garden." Bombina hadn't turned anyone into a toad since she'd promised not to nine years ago, but Parsley knew she still could. She smiled at the fairy. "Our roses are better, though."

Bombina relaxed. She marveled, as she often did, that she had given up her hobby—her art—for this lass. Bombina had felt dreadfully deprived at first, but then she'd discovered that *not* turning people into toads gave her a delightful sense of power. Since she never used up her yearly limit, she could always turn someone into a toad if she wanted to. And she still turned objects into toads, so her skills hadn't gotten rusty.

⚓ ⚓ ⚓

The next day Tansy accompanied his brothers on a ride to Snettering-on-Snoakes, and Parsley watched them in her spyglass.

They were young men now. Parsley admired how tall and straight Tansy sat in his saddle. Randolph and

111

Rudolph looked squat and awkward by comparison.

As the horses ambled along, Randolph and Rudolph argued over what color the Royal Steed should be.

"The Royal Steed must be brown," Randolph declared. "And anyone who doesn't agree is a ninny."

"Wrong!" Rudolph yelled. "The Royal Steed must be black, and you're a ninny nincompoop."

"I think," Tansy said, "that—"

"Tell him, Tansy," Randolph said. "You know I'm right."

"Tell him I'm right," Rudolph said.

"I think the Royal Steed must be taller than—"

In her spyglass Parsley saw Randolph and Rudolph turn on Tansy.

They both shouted, "You're a nitwit ninny nincompoop, and you'll never ride the Royal Steed."

I'm not a nitwit, Tansy thought. The Royal Steed can be any color, but it has to be tall, so subjects can find their sovereign. And rattles have to be tied to its knees, which will also help people locate the king. Why don't Randolph and Rudolph ever think about their subjects?

The three princes rode on in silence.

Parsley kept watching them. Turn! she thought. Come closer. Come this way. Please come.

They turned onto Rosella Lane. Parsley rushed downstairs to the library, where she threw open a window and leaned out.

She could see them, actually see them, without the spyglass! They were walking their horses down the lane. Tansy looked even nicer than he did in the spyglass, and his freckles didn't stand out quite so much. She smiled a warm, friendly smile.

Randolph and Rudolph didn't notice Parsley, but Tansy did. She seemed to be smiling at him. It was such a kind smile too, a beautiful smile, even if her teeth were as green as grass. Tansy didn't remember anyone smiling at him like that ever before.

The princes reined in their horses only a few yards from Parsley.

"The fairy Bombina lives here," Randolph announced. "A king must invite nearby fairies to a banquet every year."

"Every other year," Rudolph said. "That's quite enough."

Tansy smiled back at Parsley.

She liked his smile. Hers broadened into the loveliest, most rapturous smile ever.

Bombina came into the library carrying a bouquet of peonies from the garden. She saw Parsley's smile and became wildly jealous. Who was getting that smile? She ran to the window.

Noblemen!

Not for long. Toads!

Parsley heard Bombina and turned, a frown replacing her smile.

If Parsley had smiled at Bombina—if she hadn't frowned—

But she did frown.

Bombina decided to do the one who wasn't a twin first. She shifted her weight to her left foot, stared hard at him, and lowered her chin, still staring.

Oh no! Parsley thought. "Don't!" She leaped in front of the fairy.

Bombina found herself staring straight at Parsley.

Aaaa! Bombina tried to stop casting the spell, but it was too late.

Six

What?!! Parsley felt trapped by Bombina's gaze. She tried to squirm away from it, but she couldn't. Wind rushed by her ears, and Bombina's eyes grew bigger and bigger.

Parsley's skin pinched. Something was squeezing her harder and harder, squeezing her insides and outsides, her face and her feet and her bones and her stomach. Her ears rang and boomed.

Then it was over. Whew! She wondered if she'd looked funny while it was going on, wondered if Tansy had noticed. She turned to see.

Where was he?

Where was she?

She faced a wall that hadn't been there a second ago. It looked familiar, though. She recognized the wallpaper lily pads, but they were much too big.

Then she knew. She looked down at herself. She was chartreuse! She was a Biddlebum Toad!

She looked way way up and saw Bombina's horrified face.

See what your transformations got you, Parsley thought angrily. She wanted to scream and wail. But she didn't make a sound. She didn't know what she'd do if a croak came out of her.

Oh no! Bombina thought, feeling dizzy. Parsley will never smile at me again.

Bombina saw the three princes gawking at her, so she pulled the window shut. Then she drew the drapes, being careful not to step on poor Parsley.

Her darling was so tiny and ugly. Bombina couldn't stand to look at her. Sadly, even tragically, the fairy hiccuped twice.

Parsley vanished.

In Rosella Lane Tansy shook his head to clear it. Where had the smiling maiden gone? What had the fairy done with her?

Bombina flew to the fairy queen's palace and begged an audience with her. As soon as she saw Anura, she began to weep, although she'd never wept in all her three thousand seven hundred and fourteen years. Between sobs she blurted out the whole tale.

"Please do something. You can punish me. You can lock me up. Only let me see Parsley's human smile once more." She wiped her tears. "Toads don't have lips or teeth. Did I ever tell you what beautiful green teeth my Parsley had?"

"My poor Bombina," Anura said. "You have reaped the bitter rewards of your folly."

Bombina nodded, tears streaming.

"It would give me the greatest pleasure to help you. But you know that the only way dear Bayleaf can—"

"Her name is Parsley," Bombina wailed.

"Yes, of course. But there is only one way your Paprika—"

"Parsley!"

"Sorry! But there is just one way your little, er, maiden can resume her human shape. And that is if some other human proposes marriage to her."

Bombina smiled through her tears. How could she have forgotten? All she had to do—

"No, my poor wretched Bombina. You cannot force a young man to propose, and the little toad cannot reveal what happened to her and what the remedy is. The proposal must be of the man's free will, or it will not transform anything."

⚓ ⚓ ⚓

Parsley discovered that toads could cry. Or once-human toads could, anyway.

Oh, why had Bombina broken her promise?

She wept for a full hour. Then she looked around. She was on the bank of a wide stream. A few yards away a rotting bridge crossed the water. Ferns and a weeping willow grew along the stream bank. Beyond them was a field of tall grasses. If Parsley had been at her human height, she would have seen goats grazing in the distance.

Parsley wondered what she'd eat here. There was no parsley.

Her tongue whipped out and caught a fly. She blinked and swallowed.

Ugh! she thought. I ate an insect! It tasted sweet. She started crying again. I won't do that twice. I'll starve first.

Her tongue snaked out and snagged a mosquito.

She blinked and swallowed.

The mosquito was salty. Parsley stopped crying. Maybe she had been wrong to limit herself to parsley for all those years. She wondered how an ant would taste.

Seven

When the twins and Tansy returned to Biddle Castle from Snettering-on-Snoakes, King Humphrey IV sent for them. He rose from his throne and hugged Randolph. Or maybe it was Rudolph. He could never tell them apart. He knew about the difference in the size of their nostrils, but he could never remember which big nostril belonged to which twin.

He didn't hug Tansy.

"Lads!" He beamed at the twins and frowned at Tansy, hoping the boy wouldn't break anything just by standing still. "We were thinking about which of you should be our heir."

Randolph and Rudolph glared at each other. Tansy's heart started to pound.

"We have two stalwart sons to choose between."

Tansy's heart stopped pounding.

"So we have contrived a contest. The son who fetches us one hundred yards of linen fine enough to go through our Royal Ring"—King Humphrey IV took a ring off his pinky—"will wear this medallion." He reached into the pocket of his new Royal Ceremonial Robe and pulled out a golden medallion on which was inscribed *His Highness's Heir*. This was the cleverest part of the plan. Soon he'd know which twin was which. "The winner will rule when we are gone, and all Biddle will do his bidding."

Tansy's heart started to pound again. The contest meant trouble! Rudolph wouldn't stand for it if Randolph won, and Randolph wouldn't stand for it if Rudolph won. Whoever won, there would be trouble in Biddle.

"Father?"

King Humphrey IV scowled at Tansy. "Yes?"

"Can I seek the linen too?"

King Humphrey IV considered how peaceful home would be if Tansy were away. "You may." But he'd never let the lad rule Biddle, not even if Tansy's linen could pass through a ream of pinky rings.

Parsley spent an enjoyable afternoon sampling insects. Fleas were spicy. Ticks were sour. Midges tickled pleasantly as they went down, and caterpillars happened to taste a lot like parsley.

Late in the day a goatherd drove her goats across the stream. Parsley hid under the bridge, terrified of being trampled.

When the goats had all crossed, the goatherd sat on the far bank and dangled her feet in the stream.

Was I ever that big? Parsley wondered. She hopped backward, feeling nervous. She could be squashed so easily.

The goatherd saw the movement. She waded across the stream and groped through the ferns under the bridge. "A toad!" She picked Parsley up and placed her on her enormous palm. "Perhaps more than a toad. Kind sir, speak to me!" She waited. "Perhaps you can't talk. But you can hear my sad tale. I am not truly a goatherd." She sighed, and the wind from the sigh almost knocked Parsley off her perch. "I have been transformed."

"I AM NOT TRULY A GOATHERD."

You too? Parsley thought. Were you once a toad?

"In my true form I am a princess, Princess Alyssa-tissaprincissa."

To Parsley's horror Princess Alyssatissaprincissa brought her huge face right up to Parsley. Parsley's right eye looked at a pimple as big as a bumblebee. Then Princess Alyssatissaprincissa kissed Parsley's side. The suction of the kiss pulled her skin away from her ribs.

After the kiss Princess Alyssatissaprincissa waited a moment and then dropped Parsley. She slogged back across the stream, muttering about the scarcity of frog princes.

The ferns cushioned Parsley's fall. She lay still, catching her breath.

⚓ ⚓ ⚓

Bombina spent the day knocking her knees together to enhance her vision and her hearing. She finally saw Parsley crouching under a fern and looking like any other chartreuse Biddlebum Toad, except for a faint sparkle that only a fairy could detect.

It was too sad to bear. Bombina had to look away.

I'll never be jealous again and I'll never turn anything into a toad again, she thought, not even so much as a needle or a beetle. That will be my punishment.

⚓ ⚓ ⚓

Early the next morning King Humphrey IV saw his sons off. "Return in a week," he said.

Randolph and Rudolph each climbed into his own Royal Carriage. Tansy mounted his mare, Bhogs, whose name stood for Brown Horse of Good Speed.

When they reached Snottering on Snoakes, the villagers lined the road to see them off, and Bombina watched from her palace. She recognized the princes and itched to turn them into toads. If it hadn't been for them, Parsley would still be human. But she kept her promise and let them go by.

A mile beyond the village the road forked. The Royal Road continued to the left and wound through the principal towns of Biddle on its way to Kulornia. The right fork was Biddle Byway, which meandered through tiny villages and hamlets and never arrived anywhere.

Randolph and Rudolph took the left fork. Tansy

started to follow them. But then he pulled Bhogs up short and turned her onto Biddle Byway.

If I stick with them, he thought, and we find the perfect length of linen, who'll get it? No—who won't get it? Me.

Eight

By the end of her first day as a toad, Parsley had eaten seven fleas, twelve ticks, two spiders, a worm, a caterpillar, four gnats, and eleven midges. Then she'd gone to sleep. When she woke up late the next morning, she was surprised all over again that she was a toad. She stayed still and thought about the advantages and disadvantages of her new state.

On the plus side was diet. Bugs were scrumptious! But that was about it for the plus side.

On the minus side was the goatherd Princess Alyssatissa whatever the rest of her name was. Also on the minus side were the loss of her spyglass and the loss of Tansy in her spyglass.

And she missed Bombina. She remembered Bombina's magic tricks and how exciting it had been, especially when she was little, to live with a fairy. She remembered being disappointed when Bombina had said that only magical creatures could make magic.

Parsley's pulse quickened. She was a magical creature now.

What could she try?

Bombina began all her spells by standing on her left foot, so Parsley tried to do the same. But balancing on one foot was hard. Her shape was all wrong for it. She struggled for twenty minutes before she finally managed it and stood, wobbling a little for ten whole seconds. Then she started to go over, and she had to hop three times, while her head nodded and wagged, before she got steady again.

A silver lady's comb appeared in the air before her and fell into the moss at her feet.

She'd done it! Accidentally, but she'd done it. Too bad she had no hair.

She started to topple again. She frowned and hopped back two steps, stumbled, and got back onto her left foot.

A crock of brown boot polish landed next to the comb.

Parsley meant to laugh, but it came out as a croak, her first croak. It was a warm and melodious sound. She liked it and croaked again. She extended her four legs and stood tall and croaked again. The pitch was a trifle lower that way. She sat back to try to raise the pitch, but before she could open her mouth again, she found herself rising into the air, eighteen inches at least. She flew across the stream and crash-landed on the opposite bank.

She lay still. Gadzooks! Making magic was fun!

⚓ ⚓ ⚓

On the first morning of the contest, Tansy passed through the hamlets of Harglepool, Flambow-under-Gree, Lower Vudwich, and Craugh-over-Pughtughlouch. In the afternoon he passed through Snug Podcoomb, Woolly Podooomb, Podcoomb-upon-Hare, Upper Squeak, Lower Squeak, Popping Squeak, and Swinn-out-of-Crubble.

Wherever he went, Tansy asked Biddlers how they thought Biddle should be ruled, and he looked at linen. Each hamlet had its own master weaver, but not one of them could weave linen fine enough to

". . . AND CRASH-LANDED ON THE
OPPOSITE BANK."

squeeze through a bracelet, let alone a ring. Tansy worried that he would have found better cloth if he'd taken the Royal Road with his brothers.

Meanwhile, Randolph and Rudolph passed through towns with important-sounding short names like Ooth, Looth, Quibly, Eels, Hork, and Moowich. In Ooth the twins stopped at the first master weaver's shop they saw. The weaver pulled down his finest bolts of linen to show them.

"Hmm," Randolph said, "that one might do." He picked up a corner of cloth.

"Yes, it might." Rudolph picked up the other corner and glared at his brother.

"I saw it first." Randolph pulled the linen away from Rudolph.

"No, you didn't." Rudolph grabbed his corner again and yanked.

The linen tore down the middle.

"What have you done?" the weaver yelled. He wouldn't let the twins leave his store until one of them bought the ruined fabric, even though it didn't come close to fitting through a pinky ring. Randolph wound up paying, since he had touched the cloth first. His footman loaded it into his carriage.

There were fourteen master weavers in Ooth, and by the time the twins' carriages rolled out of town, seven bolts of torn linen were in each carriage. And not one square foot of cloth was fine enough to go through a pinky ring.

⚓ ⚓ ⚓

Parsley spent the afternoon learning to make magic. She made mistakes at first and created a big pile of objects that a toad didn't need, like a frying pan, a bow and arrows, and a bass fiddle.

But finally, she figured out how to make blue and pink and yellow balloons appear over the stream. They were a lovely sight, dozens of them, drifting over the water in friendly flocks.

By sundown she'd learned how to make almost anything she wanted, including a sprig of parsley, which had tasted awful. She'd taught herself how to make things vanish too. It was simple. All she had to do was hiccup twice, just as Bombina used to. She'd also perfected her flying, and even more important, she'd discovered how to land. She'd learned to knock her knees into her belly in order to see or hear anywhere in Biddle. She looked at Biddle Castle immediately, but she couldn't find Tansy or his horrible brothers there.

There was one bit of magic she couldn't perform, though. No matter what she tried, she couldn't turn herself back into a human.

Nine

$\mathcal{B}$ombina peeked at Parsley while Parsley was making magic. She hadn't known that her toads could do that. Hah! she thought proudly. I bet Parsley is the only one smart enough to figure it out.

⚓ ⚓ ⚓

At dusk Princess Alyssatissaprincissa came by with her goats. "Oh, Sir Toad," she called, "Your Royal Highness, where are you?"

Uh-oh! Parsley decided to fly out of danger. She stood tall and croaked. But before she could finish the spell, Princess Alyssatissaprincissa picked her up.

"I apologize, Your Majesty. I didn't know the right way before. Now I'll turn you back into a prince in no time." She hurled Parsley into the side of the bridge.

Oof! Parsley landed in a patch of dirt. *Yow!* She wondered if her back was broken. She lay still and tried not to cry.

Princess Alyssatissaprincissa waded into the stream. Just a toad, she thought, just a stupid toad.

After Princess Alyssatissaprincissa had gone, Parsley sat up carefully. Her back wasn't broken, but she was sore all over. For the first time she understood why Bombina turned people into toads.

⚓ ⚓ ⚓

Days passed. Randolph and Rudolph fought over linen in twenty towns. They hired extra carriages to carry all the cloth they had to buy. But none of it would pass through a pinky ring.

Tansy had no better luck. In Woolly Podcoomb he bought the best bolt of linen he saw, hoping it was better than anything his brothers had found.

The sixth day of the contest dawned sunny and hot. Tansy purchased an apple in the hamlet of Whither Prockington and looked at linen. In Thither Prockington he looked at more linen. He was surprised, two miles farther along, to come upon Hither

Prockington, which wasn't on any of the maps in the Royal Library. But Hither Prockington didn't have any fine linen either.

He rode on. After an hour he came to a stream.

Parsley saw the horse and rider coming and hopped under the bridge. Tansy let Bhogs drink and slipped off her back to stretch his legs.

"It's you!" Parsley cried—and discovered that she could speak.

Tansy thought he'd heard a voice, but he didn't see anyone.

Parsley hopped toward him. "Prince Tansy! Your Highness!" She wished she could hop faster. He was only a few yards away, but that was a fair distance now. She thought of flying, but she didn't want to startle him more than he was about to be startled.

Tansy was sure a maiden was calling him. Was she hiding under the bridge? He started toward it.

"Pray watch your feet."

He stood still.

"Look down, Your Highness."

A chartreuse Biddlebum Toad blinked up at him. A talking toad! Was he bewitched?

"I'm so glad to see you." Parsley tried to curtsy and almost toppled. "Especially without your wicked brothers."

Tansy gasped and fell back a step.

"They're lying snitching stinkers."

It's the heat, Tansy thought. I'm hearing things. He rushed to the stream and dunked his head. The cold water felt good.

Parsley hopped down to the stream.

Tansy stood up. He felt his mind clear. He wouldn't hear any talking animals now.

"In truth, I hate your brothers."

The toad again! He *was* bewitched.

"In truth, I admire you. I admire you so."

There she was, chartreuse and warty and smiling at him. Such a nice smile. Something in his heart fluttered.

⚓ ⚓ ⚓

Bombina saw Tansy with Parsley. It was that prince again! She began to feel jealous, but she stopped herself. She had sworn not to, and she'd keep her oaths from now on.

"THERE SHE WAS, CHARTREUSE
AND WARTY AND SMILING AT HIM."

Maybe the prince would be good for something. After all, her Parsley's smile was still the sweetest most adorable sight there was. Maybe . . .

⚓ ⚓ ⚓

Tansy sat on the riverbank and moaned. "I'm bewitched."

"No, you're not." Parsley opened her mouth to tell him about her transformation, but the words wouldn't come. She croaked to clear her throat and tried again, but she still couldn't. She stood on her left leg, spun around, and hopped twice, hoping to get some magic going, but nothing happened.

He watched her. He'd never seen a toad spin before.

She gave up. "You're not bewitched, Your Highness. I'm a talking toad." Maybe this would convince him. "If you were bewitched, you'd hear your horse speak too, wouldn't you?"

Perhaps she was right. He went to Bhogs, who was grazing near the weeping willow. "Bhogs, speak to me. Am I bewitched?"

Bhogs switched her tail and went on grazing, which meant either she couldn't speak or she didn't have anything to say. Either way, he could still be bewitched.

"If you were bewitched, the fish would be talking to you, and so would the dragonflies and the caterpillars and the"—Parsley's tongue snaked out. She snagged a gnat and swallowed it—"and the gnats and the . . ."

Maybe he was only a little bewitched, just enough to understand Toad.

Parsley decided to change the subject. "What brings you here, Prince Tansy?"

He didn't want to be rude and not answer, even if he was only imagining that the toad was speaking. If there really was a toad.

He sat again. "My father has set a contest for my brothers and me." He told her about the test and the prize. "The linen I bought isn't nearly good enough."

"I can help you!" Oh, it was wonderful to be a magical creature! "I can give you linen fine enough to go through the eye of a needle."

"If only you really could." He sighed.

Parsley felt irritated. How could she prove herself? She couldn't. He wouldn't believe the linen she made was real, no matter what. But maybe he'd believe it when his father gave him that golden medallion.

She had an idea. "Close your eyes, Your Highness."

Tansy closed his eyes, certain that when he opened them, he'd see a length of perfect linen. Perfect, but imaginary.

Parsley balanced on her left foot, feeling nervous. She had to get this just right. She tapped her nose with the fourth and last finger or toe of her right hand or front foot. Then she bent over and tapped her chin on the ground. Next she croaked at the highest pitch she could manage. And it worked.

"You can open your eyes."

Tansy did, and there, on the ground near his knee, was about three inches of coarse dirty linen.

Ten

Parsley tried not to laugh at Tansy's astonished face. "Put the linen in your saddlebag, Your Highness, and be sure it doesn't fall out."

"Thank you." Feeling silly, Tansy put the useless cloth on top of the bolt he'd purchased. "I must be going." He mounted Bhogs and galloped off without looking back.

"Farewell, dear Prince Tansy."

He shuddered and rode on. When he reached Biddle Castle, servants were unloading bolt after bolt of fabric from Randolph's and Rudolph's carriages. He took his saddlebag and followed the servants to the throne room.

King Humphrey IV was surrounded by a sea of cloth. He didn't know why the lads had carried so much home and why all of it was torn, and why none of it was nice enough to wipe his nose on.

"I have better linen somewhere, Father," Randolph said desperately. "I don't know where it's gotten to."

"I have better linen too," Rudolph said. "I don't know where mine has gotten to."

As soon as he saw the torn cloth, Tansy knew that his brothers had fought over every bolt. But most of it still looked better than the stuff he had.

King Humphrey IV said, "You lads are disappointing duffers."

"Father?" Tansy said. "I have linen too." He knelt before the throne and opened his saddlebag.

And the softest, creamiest linen he'd ever seen billowed out.

What? Tansy thought. Where's the scrap the toad gave me? Am I imagining this cloth? His fingers trembled as he drew it out.

"Let us see." Frowning, King Humphrey IV reached for the cloth. He didn't want Tansy to win, but the fabric was the finest he had ever touched. "Superb, son. Sublime."

There *had* been a toad! A magical talking toad.

"It will pass through the eye of a needle, Sire," Tansy

said. He'd won! He was going to be king. King of Biddle!

"There's my cloth," Randolph said, "the cloth that I was searching for."

"There's *my* cloth," Rudolph said.

Together they said, "Tansy stole it."

⚓ ⚓ ⚓

Parsley saw and heard it all, and she hopped up and down in fury. But she dared not fly to Tansy's aid. No one would believe a toad, and Randolph or Rudolph would step on her.

⚓ ⚓ ⚓

"I didn't steal anything!" Tansy said. "I wouldn't."

King Humphrey IV was confused. Tansy probably had filched the fabric. But from which brother? The king looked back and forth from one twin to the other until he was dizzy, but he couldn't tell.

"We shall have another contest." King Humphrey IV paced, threading his way between the mountains of material. Hmm . . . What should it be? he wondered. Hmm . . .

He had it! His grandfather, King Humphrey III, had failed at this quest and had brought home that frightful flea instead.

"Whoever brings us a dog small enough to fit in a walnut shell shall win the throne." There.

Tansy kept protesting that he'd already won until King Humphrey IV said that if he didn't shut up, he wouldn't be allowed to take part in the new contest.

He did shut up, and he set out again with his brothers the next morning. Even though he was angry at his father and the twins, he was glad to be going back to the toad. He wanted to thank her and to apologize for not believing in her. And, of course, he wanted to ask for her help again, to beg for it, if he had to.

At the fork in the road outside Snettering-on-Snoakes, Randolph's carriage and Rudolph's carriage followed Bhogs onto the Biddle Byway.

They mustn't follow me! Tansy thought. One of them might step on the toad and squash her. Or they'd fight over the little dog and hurt it, or one of them would grab it and race home.

Tansy and the twins reached Hargle-pool. Tansy

was trying to figure out how to slip away when he saw puppies playing outside a rickety shed. He made out the shapes of more puppies inside, and he saw a sign—*Best Barkers in Biddle. Ten pence per puppy*.

Some of the pups were tiny. Maybe Randolph and Rudolph could find their dogs here and stop following him.

He tied Bhogs up outside the shed. The carriages rumbled to a stop. Tansy began to go into the shed, but Randolph and then Rudolph pushed past him. He went in behind them.

A woman was sitting on a stool and combing a small dog in her lap.

Randolph said, "Harrumph—"

Rudolph said, "Harrumph, my fine woman—"

Randolph said, "Show me your smallest dog."

Rudolph said, "Show *me* your smallest dog." He glared at Randolph and stamped his foot. The whole shed shook.

Randolph glared at Rudolph.

Tansy tiptoed out of the shed.

Eleven

Tansy galloped along the Biddle Byway and finally reached Parsley's stream. He tied Bhogs to the willow and walked slowly and carefully toward the bridge. "Oh, Mistress Toad," he called

When he came close, Parsley said, "Here I am, Your Highness."

Tansy knelt down. "I apologize for not believing in you. Thank you for helping me, Mistress Toad."

"My name is Parsley, Highness. You're welcome, but I didn't help as much as I'd hoped. You've been most unfairly treated."

"You know!"

"Certainly. You won the contest, and you have to win the next one too. For Biddle's sake." She beamed up at him. "You'd be our best king ever."

That ravishing smile! His heart fluttered again.

He blushed and mumbled, "I'd try to be, Parsley."

"You *would* be. If you finally win—"

"I don't think I'll win, unless you help me again. I need—"

"A dog small enough to fit in a walnut." Parsley nodded. "I'll be happy to help."

She had him close his eyes while she made the most charming teensy-weensy dog—curly brown fur with a black patch on its back. Then she hid it.

"Open your eyes."

Tansy saw a coconut in the tall grass.

"Crack it carefully when you get home. The dog's name is Tefaw, which stands for Tiny Enough for a Walnut."

Tansy placed the coconut in his saddle-bag and thanked Parsley at least a dozen times.

She was embarrassed and changed the subject. "If you won and became king, what would you do?"

Tansy sat down. She squatted next to his right hand and never took her eyes off his face.

"I would build small Royal Glass Hills all over Biddle for children to slide down. I'd breed thousands of fireflies and release them for light on dark nights.

And every year I'd give a Best Biddler Award in three categories: interesting dreams, knowledge of Biddle history, and acrobatics."

Parsley loved Tansy's plans, and she had some ideas of her own, like letting subjects go on quests and putting their discoveries in the Royal Museum of Quest Souvenirs, or like having the Royal Army build chicken coops for people's chickens during peace-time.

Parsley and Tansy talked for hours. When the goatherd Princess Alyssatissaprincissa came by, Parsley made a big haystack and hid herself and Tansy inside it.

✤ ✤ ✤

Bombina watched them talk. Keep smiling, Parsley, she thought. Smile, my love.

✤ ✤ ✤

Tansy liked Parsley's smile more and more, until he believed that toads were the most beautiful creatures in Biddle. And the smartest and the friendliest.

For her part Parsley admired Tansy more and more.

And when he said he'd make toads the Royal Animal and make people pay a fine for squashing them, her heart almost burst with love.

Night came. Tansy stretched out under the bridge, and Parsley settled down a yard or two away, in case he rolled over in his sleep.

They talked the whole next day and the day after that and the day after that, for six days, until Tansy had to return to Biddle Castle.

While he saddled Bhogs, he tried to say how much it had meant to him to talk to her, but he couldn't find the words. He mounted Bhogs and looked down at Parsley. "Thank you, and farewell." He rode off, turning to wave until he could no longer distinguish her from the grass.

Twelve

Tansy heard barking as soon as he crossed the Royal Drawbridge. In the throne room puppies were chewing on the Royal Drapes, making messes on the Royal Rug, leaping at Royal Chair Legs and Royal Table Legs and the Royal Legs of Randolph and Rudolph. King Humphrey IV was standing on his throne, lifting his new Royal Ceremonial Robe out of reach.

None of the puppies was small enough to fit in a walnut shell.

"I had a smaller dog somewhere, Father," Randolph said.

"I had a smaller dog too," Rudolph said.

"Remove these puppies," King Humphrey IV roared.

Royal Servants shooed the dogs from the room.

King Humphrey IV descended and sat on his throne.

Tansy knelt down. "I have a dog too." He took out the coconut. Using his hunting knife, he cracked it carefully and found a walnut shell inside. He began to smile as he cracked the walnut shell—and found a peanut shell. That Parsley! Grinning broadly, he cracked the peanut shell and found a pistachio shell, and inside the pistachio shell was Tefaw. The dog pranced around on Tansy's hand and barked an astonishingly deep bark for such a tiny creature.

"There it is," Randolph said. "There's my dog."

"There's *my* dog," Rudolph said.

Together they said, "Tansy stole it."

"I did not steal it!" Tansy yelled. "I got it my—"

"Did too steal it," Randolph hollered.

"Did too steal it," Rudolph screamed.

King Humphrey IV was puzzled. The twins had never lied before. But Tansy did look truthful, and they hadn't said a word about a coconut.

There was only one thing to do. "We will have a final contest. The son who brings home the most beautiful bride will be our heir." The twins would hardly be able to say they'd misplaced a maiden.

"I HAVE A DOG TOO."

Parsley was angrier than she'd ever been before. Tansy won, she thought, fuming. Fair and square.

⚓ ⚓ ⚓

Bombina wondered why Parsley looked so angry. The fairy watched and waited.

⚓ ⚓ ⚓

Randolph and Rudolph didn't try to follow Tansy this time. Their carriages turned onto the Royal Road and sped on.

Tansy kicked Bhogs into a gallop. He didn't know what to do. He didn't want to pick a bride just because she was pretty.

Bhogs streaked through Harglepool.

The kindest queen in Biddle history was Queen Lorelei, and her nose had been a bit too big. And although Queen Sonora had been beautiful, she was remembered for her wisdom.

Bhogs dashed through Lower Vudwich.

Besides, no matter how pretty his choice was, his father would probably say Randolph's or Rudolph's choice was prettier.

Bhogs flew though Podcoomb-upon-Hare.

And what if he won and had to marry a maiden he didn't like?

Bhogs tore through Popping Squeak.

He didn't know what to do. The only thing he knew was that he wanted to discuss it with Parsley.

If only he could find a maiden as smart as she was— as smart and sweet and understanding, with a smile that was even half as heartwarming.

There was her stream. He slid off Bhogs's back. "Parsley, where are you?"

She was so happy to see him. She put all her happiness into her smile.

As soon as Tansy saw the smile, he knew. He couldn't marry anyone but Parsley, even if she was a toad. He had to marry his love, if she'd have him.

He dropped to his knees. "Parsley, will you marry me?"

⚓ ⚓ ⚓

Bombina whooped and yelled, "He did it! My precious Parsley! I love that prince!"

For a moment Parsley just blinked up at Tansy. Her smile froze. Wind rushed by her ears. She'd felt this wind before. What???

Oh no oh no. Her skin was expanding. She was pulsing all over, her insides, her head. *Boom! Boom!* It hurt! And her blood was rushing, swooshing, flooding.

Tansy's dear face, coming closer, looking frightened. And now she was above his head, rising higher. Oh oh oh!

It was over.

Parsley panted, her hand pressed to her chest.

Her hand! She had a hand?

She looked down at herself. She was human again!

It's the maiden from the fairy's palace, Tansy thought, the one with green teeth.

Tansy saved me! Parsley thought. She smiled down at him. "Of course I'll marry you, if you still want me."

"I do!" He could see his beloved toad in her smile and in her eyes.

She said, "Do you like parsley?"

Thirteen

Randolph and Rudolph each decided that it didn't matter who they thought was the most beautiful maiden. It only mattered what their father thought.

On the outskirts of Ooth Randolph saw a pretty maiden picking roses in her garden. He stopped his carriage and got out.

Rudolph got out of his carriage.

"I say," Randolph said, "will you marry me if my father the king chooses me to be his heir and chooses you as the most beautiful bride?"

Rudolph said, "Will you marry *me* if the king chooses me to be his heir and chooses you as the most beautiful bride?"

"I asked her first," Randolph yelled.

"I asked her second," Rudolph shouted.

The maiden giggled. She pointed to each of them in turn and said,

"Which son?
Either one.
Pink, gold, blue.
I choose you!"

She pointed at Randolph.

He smirked at Rudolph and climbed back into his carriage. The maiden climbed in after him. The carriages rolled on.

Whenever Randolph and Rudolph passed a pretty maiden, they stopped their carriages and each asked her to marry him if King Humphrey IV chose him as heir and chose her as most beautiful.

Some maidens picked Randolph. Some picked Rudolph. Some refused them both and said,

"Which son?
Neither one.
Pink, gold, gray.
I say nay!"

By the time they reached Moowich, each twin had ten carriages full of maidens.

⚓ ⚓ ⚓

Tansy and Parsley and Bhogs ambled down the Biddle Byway. At the end of the week they reached Biddle Castle. As soon as she saw it, Parsley felt nervous. She wanted to win the throne for Tansy, but she didn't think she was pretty enough.

In the throne room Randolph's maidens were milling about on the right side of the room, and Rudolph's were milling about on the left. There were scores of them. King Humphrey IV was glad to see so many winsome wenches, but what kind of kings would the twins be if they couldn't make up their minds about which maiden to marry?

Tansy entered holding Parsley's hand. He led her to the throne, and they both knelt down.

"Father, this is Parsley, the most beautiful maiden in Biddle, the maiden I wish to marry."

"Let us look at you, lass."

Parsley blushed and smiled at King Humphrey IV.

"She's hideous!" Randolph screamed. "Look at her teeth."

"Look at her teeth!" Rudolph shrieked. "She's horrendous!"

No one saw Bombina materialize behind Rudolph's maidens. Luckily for the twins, she didn't hear what they'd just said.

King Humphrey IV noticed the color of the damsel's teeth, but he paid more attention to the loveliness of her smile. With such a smile her teeth could be sprouting fur and he wouldn't mind.

"Sire!" Randolph hissed. "Think of your ripped Royal Robe."

"Sire!" Rudolph hissed. "Think of your broken scepter."

King Humphrey IV frowned. He looked over at Randolph's lasses and beckoned to one of them. He beckoned to a beauty of Rudolph's too. They approached, and each of them was at least as pretty as Parsley.

"Oh no you don't!" Bombina belowed. She marched to the throne. She wouldn't turn the king into a toad, but she'd turn him into something.

A fairy! King Humphrey IV trembled. He stood

and bowed. Randolph and Rudolph trembled. They bowed too.

Tansy gasped. She was the one who'd turned Parsley into a toad! Well, she wasn't going to do it again. He drew his sword.

Parsley ran into Bombina's arms. "I missed you!" She smiled up at the fairy.

Tansy sheathed his sword.

Bombina felt dizzy. Her Parsley was smiling at her again. She began to weep happy tears. "Oh my dear!"

King Humphrey IV thought, The damsel is dear to a fairy? A fairy's friend would make a fine future queen. He cleared his throat. "Tansy shall be our heir."

Tansy could hardly believe it. He was going to be king, and he was going to marry his love. He felt overjoyed, overjoyed in a solemn way. He'd be a fair and kind king, and he'd make sure his subjects always had enough bathwater and mittens and—

Randolph screeched, "But I have to be king!"

Rudolph screeched, "But I have to be king!"

Randolph yelled, "Tansy broke the scepter and he tore—"

Parsley said, "He did not! You both did it and blamed him."

"They did?" King Humphrey IV looked at the twins. Could this be true? The fairy would know. "Did they?"

Tansy held his breath.

Bombina stared at each twin in turn and used her fairy powers to find out. She nodded. "They did." She felt a thrill. Randolph and Rudolph would make superb toads. She stared at Randolph.

"No!" Parsley yelled.

Bombina stopped staring. "No?"

Parsley considered. Randolph and Rudolph deserved to be toads if anyone did. But Princes Alyssatissaprincissa might propose to one of them, and then he would be a prince all over again. She had an idea. She whispered it to Bombina, who nodded.

The fairy flapped her wings twice, and howled *weejoon zowowow ay yay ay.*

Epilogue

Randolph and Rudolph spun around faster and faster, so fast that they created a tornado in the throne room, and all the pretty maidens wept and whimpered.

At last the twins stopped spinning, and two goatherds stood glaring at each other. Bombina hiccuped twice, and they vanished, one appearing in a meadow just north of Princess Alyssatissaprincissa and the other appearing in a meadow just east of Princess Alyssatissaprincissa.

Parsley and Tansy were married the next day. King Humphrey IV conducted the ceremony, and Bombina gave away the bride. Zeke and Nelly were there, along with Parsley's younger brother, Pepper.

Eventually Randolph married Princess Alyssatissaprincissa, and Rudolph married the princess's sister, Countess Marianabanessacontessa, who was also a goatherd. Having their own separate herds of goats pleased the twins, and they came to like each other.

Bombina never turned anyone into a toad again, but she performed thousands of other magic tricks for Tansy and Parsley's children, who all inherited their mother's captivating smile.

Tansy was a wonderful king. He put his subjects first, and he rode a tall horse so they were always able to find him. His subjects loved having their own souvenirs in the Royal Museum of Quest Souvenirs, and his subjects' chickens loved the coops the Royal Army built for them.

Bombina's cook taught Parsley's favorite parsley recipes to the Royal Cook, and the Royal Cook invented a few of her own. Parsley's smile grew greener and greener, and she never ate another insect.

And they all, monarchs and subjects and goatherds and fairies, lived happily ever after.

The Fairy's
Return

Love to Betsy and Ben and Amy and
Sean and their animal pals

—G.C.L.

One

Once upon a time in the kingdom of Biddle a baker's son and a princess fell in love. This is how it came about—

Robin, the baker's son, rode to Biddle Castle in the back of the bakery cart. His older brothers, Nat and Matt, sat on the driver's bench with their father, Jake, who was a poet as well as a baker.

Robin began a joke. "What's a dwarf's—"

"Son," Jake said,

"A joker is a fool,
Who never went to a place of learning."

Nat said, "Jokers are dottydaftish." He had a knack for inventing words.

Matt said, "Jokes are dumdopety." He had a knack for inventing words too.

Robin hated being thought stupid. "Jokes aren't dumb or dopey, and I'm not dotty or daft. If you'd ever listen to a whole joke, you'd see." If they did, they'd realize that jokers were just as smart as poets and word inventors.

Jake just shook his head. Robin was the first moron in family history. Not only did he make up jokes, he also gave things away. Why only a week ago, on the lad's eleventh birthday to be exact, Robin had given a roll to a beggar. For free!

Generosity was against family policy. Jake had told his sons repeatedly never to give anyone something for nothing. He had learned this from his own father, a genius who could make up three poems at once.

The bakery cart rumbled across the Biddle Castle drawbridge. At the door to the Royal Kitchen, Jake reined in their nag, Horsteed, who had been named by Nat.

When all the bread had been carried into the kitchen, Jake began to chat with the Royal Chief Cook. As Jake often said,

"A nice customer chat
Puts a coin in your bonnet."

Nat chatted with the Royal First Assistant Cook, and Matt chatted with the Royal Second Assistant Cook.

Robin began to tell his dwarf joke to the Royal Third Assistant Cook, but the Royal Third Assistant Cook interrupted with his recipe for pickled goose feet with jellied turnips.

Robin disliked jellied anything, so after he'd heard the recipe three times, he said, "How interesting. Please excuse me." He slipped out the Royal Kitchen Door and into the Royal Garden, where commoners weren't allowed.

But he didn't know that.

Two

$\mathcal{D}$ame Cloris, the Royal Governess, sat primly upright on a bench in a small meadow in the garden. Her lace cap had slipped over her face, and it fluttered as she breathed. She was fast asleep.

Princess Lark sat on the grass nearby, her favorite ball a few feet away. She wished she had someone to play with.

Yesterday had been her eleventh birthday, and her birthday party had been awful, just like every other party she'd ever had. The guests had been children of the castle nobility, and the party had begun with a game of hide-and-seek. Lark had taken the first turn as It. While she counted, she wished with all her might that this time her guests would really play with her.

But when she opened her eyes, she saw that no one

had hidden. Oh, they were pretending to hide. Aldrich, the Earl of Pildenue's son, was standing next to a tree, with one foot concealed behind it. And his sister, Cornelia, had stationed herself behind a bush that only came up to her waist.

The children wouldn't hide because they were afraid Lark would fail to find them. And not one of them dared to let a princess fail at anything.

She had told them she wouldn't mind. She had also said she wouldn't mind being It forever. But it didn't matter what she said.

The next activity, baseball, was even worse. When Lark was at bat, if she hit the ball at all—a yard, a foot, half an inch—no one tried to catch it. They thought it would be disrespectful to make a princess out, so Lark had to dash around the bases for a home run she hadn't earned.

When the other team was at bat, they tried not to hit the ball, because it would never do for their team to beat Lark's.

Lark declared the game over after one inning and declared the party over too. She ate her birthday cake alone—the single bite she was able to get down before she ran to her room, sobbing.

And now here she was, in the garden with her ball and a sleeping governess. She watched idly as Robin approached. She noticed that his jerkin was plain brown, without even the tiniest jewel. How unusual. And there was a hole in his breeches.

She sat up straight. His feet were bare. He was a commoner!

Lark had never spoken to a commoner. Maybe he'd be different.

Robin had no idea who the old lady and the lass were. He only knew the lass looked sad. Maybe a joke would cheer her up, if she'd let him tell it.

"Hello," he said. "What's a dwarf's . . ." She wasn't interrupting. He began to feel nervous. ". . . favorite food?"

She smiled up at him. He hadn't bowed, which was wonderful. But she had no idea what the answer was. The king of the dwarfs had visited Biddle last year, but she couldn't remember what he'd eaten. "Potatoes?"

Robin's heart started to pound. She was going to listen to the punch line! "No. Strawberry shortcake." He waited.

"Why straw—" Then she knew. She started laughing. A dwarf! Strawberry *short*cake!

Robin laughed too, for sheer delight. She liked the joke! He sat down next to her and tried another one. "Which rank of nobility is best at math?"

Was this another joke? "The earl?"

"No. He's earl-y and catches the worm."

She pictured Aldrich's father grubbing for worms. That was so funny.

Robin thought she had the best laugh, gurgly and tinkly. "It's the count."

Numbers! A count! She laughed harder.

Robin thought, She has a superb sense of humor.

Dame Cloris, the governess, snored, a long rattle followed by two snorts. Robin and Lark giggled.

"Why is a king like a yardstick?"

Lark tried to guess. Her father didn't look anything like a yardstick, not with his bad posture. She gave up and shrugged.

"They're both rulers."

She laughed. Rulers! The king would love it. "I can't wait to tell Father."

Robin frowned. "You're lucky. My father hates jokes.

Is your father a Royal Servant?"

He didn't know? Oh, no! As soon as she told him, he'd turn stiff and uncomfortable, just like everybody else. She thought of lying, but she didn't like to lie, and he was too nice to lie to anyway. "No. He's the king."

He blinked. "Then you're—"

She nodded. "I'm Princess Lark."

Three

Robin jumped up and bowed. A princess liked his jokes! Bowing wasn't enough. He took her hand and pumped it up and down.

Lark was delighted. Most people were afraid to touch her. "What's your name?"

"Robin."

"We both have bird names!" It was amazing.

"I wouldn't like to be named Spoonbill." He grinned. "Or Swallow. Good morning, Master Swallow. How did your breakfast go down?"

"Or my name could be Vulture. Good morning, Princess Vulture. I hate to think what you had for breakfast." She stood up. "Why doesn't your father like your jokes?"

"I don't know why."

He looks sad, Lark thought. "They're terrific jokes. How do you think of them?"

"I don't know." He blushed. "I just do."

"All the time?"

"Except when I'm unhappy or angry. Then I can't make up any. I can't even remember my old ones." He changed the subject. He didn't like to think about being jokeless. "Why is a bakery—"

Dame Cloris moaned in her sleep.

"Who's she?"

"She's Dame Cloris, my governess." Lark giggled. "She's a deep sleeper. Why is a bakery what?"

"Oh. Why is a bakery like a garden?"

Lark tried to figure it out. One was outdoors and one was indoors. That wasn't it. She stopped trying. It was more fun to let him surprise her. "I give up."

"They're both flowery." Or floury, he thought.

She chuckled. "You're clever."

That wasn't what his father and brothers thought. "My father's a baker. You should visit our bakery. It's in Snettering-on-Snoakes. You could come tomorrow." If she came, he wouldn't have to wait a week to see her again. "Or the next day." And maybe she'd make Jake and Nat and Matt listen to a joke.

"I'd like to come."

"When you do, could you order me to tell you a joke, a whole one, all the way through?"

She nodded. Nobody had ever asked for her help before. They just wanted to do things for her.

Robin could hardly wait. Everything would change when his family heard a whole joke. He loved Lark!

He was so happy, he had to do something. He picked up her ball and gave it to her. "Want to play catch?"

Did she! She threw him the ball. He threw it back. He threw hard. He didn't seem to care if she failed to catch it. This was what she'd always wanted. This was heavenly.

She was terrible at catch, since she'd never had a chance to practice. But she was happy to chase the ball and throw it back as well as she could.

Sometimes when she missed the ball, it wasn't her fault, though. He kept telling jokes and timing them so that she was laughing when he threw the ball. He was playing tricks to *make* her miss. She loved him!

The ball bounced off her arm. She and Robin ran after it, but—

Oh no! It hit Dame Cloris's skirts, right below the knee.

Dame Cloris yelped and opened her eyes. A commoner! With Princess Lark! She screamed, and then she fainted.

Lark and Robin rushed to her. Two Royal Garden Guards came on the run. One waved smelling salts under Dame Cloris's nose. The other picked Robin up by his collar and carried him away.

Robin yelled, "Don't forget! Come to the bakery."

"I'll be there."

The guard dumped Robin at the Royal Kitchen Door. "Stay out of the garden," he growled, and marched off. Robin slipped into the kitchen, where Jake and Nat and Matt were ending their customer chats.

On the way back to Snettering-on-Snoakes Robin announced, "While you were talking, I played catch with Princess Lark, and—"

"You falsfibbulator!" Nat started laughing. "That's the sillfooliest thing I ever heard!"

Matt laughed too. "It's nutcrazical!"

Jake stopped the cart. "Matt! Natt! I mean Nat! Matt! Don't make fun of Robin just because he isn't as brilliant as we are. He only *wishes* he could meet

"A COMMONER! WITH PRINCESS LARK!"

a princess and play—"

"I don't only—"

"But it's a bad wish." Jake was proud to be a commoner and wouldn't have wanted to play catch with a king.

"*Royalty and commoners must never mix.*
Remember this, or you will be in a predicament."

"She's going to come to the bakery." So there.

Jake was shocked. Robin truly believed he'd met the princess. He was too stupid to know what was real and what wasn't. He was an imbecile.

Robin repeated, "She's coming. And she likes my jokes. You'll see."

Four

In the Royal Dining Hall that evening, Lark said, "Father . . ."

"Harrumph?"

"Today I played with the lad I want to marry some day." She laughed, remembering the ruler joke.

The king smiled. His daughter had a lovely laugh, and he didn't hear it often enough. "Well, harrumph?" Meaning, *Well, who?* King Humphrey V was known far and wide as King Harrumphrey.

"He's Robin, the baker's son. He told—"

King Harrumphrey's face turned red. "You're not harrumphying any harrumpher's son!"

"I will so harrumphy him, I mean, marry him!"

"Harrumph!"

The next morning Lark told Dame Cloris that she wanted to go to Snettering-on-Snoakes.

Dame Cloris yawned. "I'm feeling too sleepy, Your

Highness. I can't go with you . . . and you can't go without me."

The following day Dame Cloris said she was still too sleepy. The day after that she was too tired, and the next day she was too sleepy again.

Lark appealed to her father. "It would be educational for me," she said. "I'd meet our subjects."

King Harrumphrey frowned. Was the baker's son behind this? "You don't have to meet any harrumphs. When the Royal Chief Councillor puts our golden harrumph on your head someday, you'll harrumph all you need in an instant."

"But Father, what if I don't harru—know all I need?"

"Sweetharrumph, trust us, commoners are harrumph. Even worse, they're harrumph."

"Please, can't I go? I won't stay long."

"No, you can't. Not for all the harrumph in Kulornia."

⚓ ⚓ ⚓

Robin was miserable when Lark didn't come to the bakery the next day or the next. He couldn't even cheer himself up with jokes, because he was too upset to think of any. And it didn't help that Nat kept calling him His Hikingness, and that Matt kept saying, "Where's your prinroycess?"

It crossed Robin's mind that Lark had only pretended to like his jokes. After all, nobody else liked them.

But she *had* liked them. He was sure of it. And she had liked him. He couldn't have imagined it.

Maybe she'd hurt herself and couldn't come. Or maybe that snooty Dame wouldn't let her come. That must have been it. He felt better and made up three jokes.

The next time they delivered bread, he'd find out what had happened. He'd tell the new jokes, and he'd get proof that they'd met. Maybe she'd write on Royal Stationery that she thought he was clever and his jokes were funny.

Most important of all, when he saw her, he'd tell her he loved her.

But Jake wouldn't take him to the castle anymore. He said,

> "*To the castle you could come*
> *If you weren't so darn moronic.*"

That made Robin mad. He wasn't moronic! And if his father wouldn't take him, he'd go on his own.

Every afternoon one of the brothers went to Snoakes Forest to chop wood for the bakery oven. Whoever it was packed a picnic lunch, took the family's ax, and set off.

When it was his turn, Robin chopped the wood as fast as he could. Then he hiked past the Sleep In Inn, through fields and low hills, and on to Biddle Castle.

On the way he thought of a dozen more jokes. The seventh was his favorite: Why do noblemen like to stare? Because they're peers.

He pictured Lark's reaction. First surprise, and then her musical laugh, which would make him feel prouder than a prince and smarter than anyone in his whole family tree.

But when Robin reached the castle, he couldn't get past the Royal Drawbridge Guard.

He tried again on his next seven turns chopping wood. Sometimes the Royal Drawbridge Guard stopped him. He got past that guard a few times, only to be stopped by the Royal Castle Door Guard or the

Royal Garden Gate Guard. Once, he managed to enter the castle, but the moment he put his foot on the Royal Grand Staircase, the Royal Grand Staircase Guard rushed at him and tossed him out as if he were a sack of flour.

Oh, Lark! Oh, love! He might never see her again, the one person in Biddle who appreciated a good joke.

Five

Two years passed, but Lark didn't forget Robin.
How could she, when he was the only one who'd ever
treated her as a normal person? How could she, when
the last time she'd laughed had been with him?

King Harrumphrey tried to make her laugh. He'd
sneak up on her and tickle her. But she'd stopped
being ticklish long ago. He'd make funny faces. They
might have made her laugh, if it hadn't been his fault
she couldn't visit Robin. So she'd scowl instead.

The king often sent the Royal Jester to amuse her.
But the jester was as afraid of offending her as everybody else. So he'd just turn cartwheels and never tell
jokes. And his cartwheels weren't that funny.

⚓ ⚓ ⚓

Two more years passed. Nat became betrothed to
Holly, the oldest of the Sleep In innkeeper's three

daughters. Matt became betrothed to the middle sister, Molly.

Robin had stopped thinking of Lark a hundred times a day. Whenever he did remember her, he concentrated on something else to keep from feeling bad.

He still hadn't succeeded in telling his family a complete joke. He would have given up, but jokes are meant to be told, and they'd pop out in spite of himself.

And he still hadn't convinced his family that he wasn't simpleminded. One day, in desperation, he gave in and tried word inventing. He said, "I may not be brillbrainiant, but I'm smarquick enough."

But Nat said, "Stupidated people always think they're keenwittish."

And Matt said, "Your words are the flimflawsiest I've ever heard."

Jake, however, thought Robin's invented words were a good sign. He began to hope that his youngest boy was finally catching up to the rest of the family.

That is, until the day Robin gave an entire muffin to the tailor. Robin was at the front of the bakery, taking coins and making change from the cash box. The tailor, who was the poorest person in

Snettering-on-Snoakes, stepped forward with a halfpenny for the leg of a gingerbread man. Robin saw him look hungrily at a blueberry muffin.

Robin glanced around. Nat was taking scones out of the oven. Matt was in the storeroom. And Jake was looking down as he rolled out dough.

Robin grabbed a blueberry muffin just as Jake raised his head. The baker watched, appalled, as Robin passed the muffin to the tailor.

"Stop!" Jake shouted.

The tailor ran out of the shop.

Jake's hopes for Robin collapsed. The lad didn't understand proper behavior. Jake repeated his rule slowly.

> *"Never ever give anything away for free,*
> *As my father said. Listen to him and to I."*

From then on Jake wouldn't let Robin do anything except knead dough, the most boring job in the bakery. Robin hated it, and he despaired of ever proving he wasn't thickheaded.

A week later Golly, the youngest of the innkeeper's

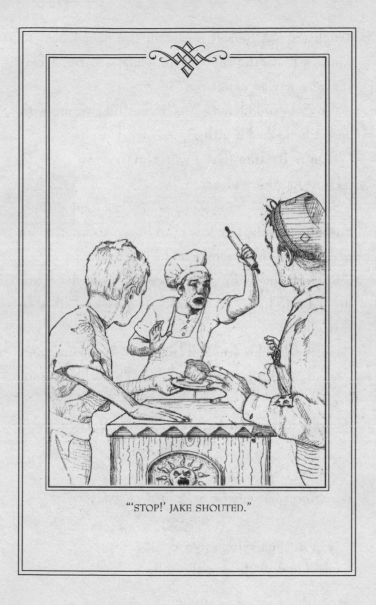

"'STOP!' JAKE SHOUTED."

daughters, sat herself down on the bench next to Robin's kneading table. She said, "Dearie, I fear you're worrying about me."

Why? he wondered. Was something wrong with her? She looked healthy.

"You're fretting that I won't marry you."

He stopped kneading.

She went on. "Some wenches may not want a stupid husband, dearie, but I do. I'm bossy, so when we're wed, I'll run the Sleep In and I'll run you."

Robin gulped. "I'm not marrying anybody." Lark flashed into his mind. Once he would have liked to marry her.

Golly poked his arm and laughed. "At the inn, your job will be fluffing up the pillows. That's like kneading, dearie."

Jake left his cake batter and came to them.

> "Son, Golly will make a fine wife,
>   Since your mind's not sharp as a dagger."

"I'm not marrying anybody."
Jake laughed along with Golly.

Six

Golly sat with Robin all morning, and she didn't stop talking for a second. She told him who would be invited to their wedding and which songs would be sung and which dances danced. She told him what jerkin to wear on the wedding day and which side to part his hair on.

He didn't knead the dough that morning. He punched it and squashed it and strangled it.

Eventually Golly left to have her lunch at the inn. Robin packed his own lunch in a basket and left too. It was his turn to chop wood, but first he needed to walk off the hours with Golly. He circled around the Sleep In so she wouldn't see him and headed for the hills and fields south of Biddle Castle.

He wasn't far from the castle when he heard someone singing in the distance. He stood still. He'd heard that voice before. He heard a deeper sound. It was familiar too. He ran toward the sounds.

When he got closer, he could hear the words to the song.

> *"O alas. O alack.*
> *O woe is me.*
> *I've lost my true love,*
> *And I'll never fly free."*

As he ran, he thought, That's odd. *Me* rhymes with *free*.

Almost a mile from Robin, Lark was sitting on the bank of Snoakes Stream. She'd pulled her skirts up to her knees and had taken off her slippers and her hose. Her feet dangled in the stream. She was feeding the ducks and singing her heart out.

> *"My love's not a widgeon,*
> *Nor a pigeon."*

Those are birds! Robin thought. He ran faster.

> *"My love's not a macaw,*
> *Nor a jackdaw."*

The voice was farther away than he'd thought. He was getting near the castle.

> *"My love's not a waterfowl,*
> *Nor a tawny owl.*
> *O alas. O alack.*
> *O woe is me.*
> *I've lost my Robin . . ."*

A robin! Me? He was out of breath, but he managed one last burst of speed.

There they were. An elderly lady with a lace cap over her face was snoring on a blanket. And Lark was on the stream bank.

> *"And we'll never fly free."*

He rushed to her. "Lark!"

She turned. "Robin?" She stood, almost losing her footing on the slippery stones in the stream. Her skirts trailed in the water. She smiled radiantly. "Robin!"

He thought of a joke. "What does the postal coach driver wear in cold weather?"

A joke! Lark hadn't felt so happy in years. "I

don't know. What?"

He'd missed her so. He hadn't realized how much till now. He forgot about the joke and just smiled at her.

Dame Cloris stirred on the blanket. In her dream King Harrumphrey was making her a countess.

Lark prompted Robin. "What?"

What what? Oh, the joke. "When it's cold out, the postal coach driver wears a coat of mail."

She thought for a second, then laughed. A coat of mail! A coat of letters!

He'd never stopped loving her, not for a minute, whether he'd known it or not.

She began to climb out of the stream, but she lost her balance. "Oh, no!" She reached out to Robin. Before he could grab her, she fell backward into the water with a big splash.

In the governess's dream, the king's sword clanged. He touched it to her forehead. "I harrumph you a Royal Harrumphess."

Robin thought Lark might be hurt. He waded in. She laughed and splashed him.

He splashed her back. She was delighted. No one else would have splashed her. She held out her hands as if she wanted him to help her up, but when he took them, she pulled him down.

Water got in his nose. He snorted and shook the hair out of his eyes. He splashed Lark again.

She laughed.

Dame Cloris's snore changed pitch. She dreamed there was a commotion at the door of the Royal Throne Room.

Lark brushed the water out of her eyes. "I missed you," she said. "I tried to go to your bakery, but nobody would let me."

She did try! "I went to the castle to find you."

"You did?"

Dame Cloris whimpered. In her dream, seven commoners strode into the throne room.

Robin said, "But I couldn't get to you. The guards kept stopping me." He took a deep breath. "I love you."

"I love you. Will you marry me?"

Robin knelt in the water. "Yes, I'll marry you. I'm honored. I'm . . ." He leaned over to kiss her hand.

In the dream the commoners chanted, "No countesses for governesses! No governesses for countesses!" Dame Cloris woke up. She opened her eyes and saw Lark and Robin in the water. She screamed.

Seven

A Royal Drawbridge Guard, his sword drawn, raced to Dame Cloris's aid.

Robin surged out of the stream and ran, calling behind him, "I love you."

Lark called back, "I love you. Remember, we're betrothed."

Dame Cloris fainted. The guard picked her up along with Lark's slippers and hose. He escorted Lark to the Royal Throne Room, where she stood in her bare feet, dripping on the Royal Tile Floor. He placed Dame Cloris on a chair. She revived and told the king what she'd witnessed.

King Harrumphrey yelled *"Harrumph!"* for a full five minutes. Lark just looked defiant.

Finally, his anger collapsed. "Larkie, why do you want to harrumphy him?"

"He makes me laugh." And he treated her like she

was an ordinary person. And she loved to be with him.

The king thought about it. There was nothing wrong with laughter. But laughing with a commoner was vulgar. Laughing with a prince was excellent.

Hmm . . . He summoned the Royal Chief Scribe. "We wish to harrumph a proclamation."

The scribe unrolled a scroll and dipped her pen in ink.

"Hear harrumph. Hear harrumph."

Hear ye. Hear ye, the scribe wrote.

"Insofar and inasharrumph that we have a har-rumphter . . ."

Insofar and inasmuch as we have a scepter . . .

"Not this harrumphter." The king raised his scepter. "That harrumphter." He pointed at Lark.

. . . daughter . . .

King Harrumphrey continued.

Lark listened, horror-struck.

"And said harrumphter, Princess Harrumph, is old harrumph to marry—"

"Father!"

He ignored her and went on.

The scribe wrote, *. . . and said daughter, Princess Lark, is old enough to marry, then let it be known that we will bestow her hand upon any . . .* She was stuck again. She thought for a moment and wrote, . . . *man who* . . . .

King Harrumphrey tapped the scroll. "Not that 'any harrumph.'"

The scribe wrote *noble* in tiny letters to the left of *man*.

The king was getting annoyed. "Not 'any harrumphman.' 'Any harrumph.'"

"He means 'any baker's son,'" Lark said.

King Harrumphrey frowned, and the scribe knew better than to write *baker's son*.

The king roared, "Harrumph! Any prince who can make said princess harrumph."

. . . *any prince who can make said princess harrumph*. The scribe crossed out *harrumph*. Happy! Must be. She wrote, *happy*.

"Not 'harrumphy.'" King Harrumphrey paused. He wanted Lark to be happy. And she would be. The proclamation would make sure of it. "Not 'harrumphy.' 'Harrumph.'"

In turn the scribe tried *wise, good at checkers, able to speak six languages, say harrumph more often, live a long time*. The scroll was getting messy, and she was

"THE KING ROARED, 'HARRUMPH!'"

going to have to copy it all over, if she ever figured out what it was supposed to say.

At last, the king shook his belly and said, "Har har har harrumph."

She got it.

Hear ye. Hear ye. Insofar and inasmuch as we have a daughter, and said daughter, Princess Lark, is old enough to marry, then let it be known that we will bestow her hand upon any prince who can make said princess laugh.

⚓ ⚓ ⚓

After he finished chopping wood, Robin returned to the bakery and started kneading again. He felt so joyful that new jokes were coming to him as fast as he could think.

Nat said, "Father has splenthrillous news, Robin."

Today's a good day for good news, Robin thought, smiling.

Jake cleared his throat and announced that Nat, Matt, and Robin would wed Holly, Molly, and Golly in two weeks. He added, "From then on,

"Nat and Matt will roll dough for the pie tin,
While Robin fluffs up pillows at the hotel."

Robin's jokes stopped coming, and he almost screamed. Golly was the last person he wanted for a wife. She didn't have a bit of Lark's sweetness, Lark's sense of humor, Lark's complete lovableness.

He took a deep breath. He was going to marry Lark. She'd tell her father about their betrothal, and then she'd come to him or send for him, or whatever royalty would do.

But what if the king didn't want him to marry her?

Well, maybe he wouldn't at first. But she'd persuade him. She'd tell him how much they loved each other. He'd understand.

Eight

Lark couldn't sleep all night. What if a real prince made her laugh? What if he told a joke almost as good as one of Robin's, and she laughed before she caught herself? She wouldn't love the prince, but she'd be stuck with him.

She worried about it till dawn. Finally she decided that she had to make herself sad, so sad there'd be no chance of a laugh, no matter what any ridiculous prince said.

While she dressed, she thought of the calamities that befell people every day. They stubbed their toes, lost their favorite hat feathers, put spoiled raspberries into their mouths, were stung by bees, misspelled words, dropped their candy in the dirt. The list was endless.

A tear trickled down her cheek.

While she waited for the first prince to come, she

read tragedies in the Royal Library. Within a few days she was weeping steadily. She cried herself to sleep at night and woke up crying in the morning.

King Harrumphrey hated to see her cry. It made him feel like crying too. He would have done almost anything to make his Larkie happy. Anything but let her marry a commoner.

A week before Robin's wedding to Golly, the first prince arrived at Biddle Castle. He was taken to the Royal Tournament Arena to perform before an audience of Lark, King Harrumphrey, Dame Cloris, the Royal Councillors, and any Royal Nobles who wanted to come. No commoners allowed.

The prince juggled cheeses while a mouse stood on his head. The councillors and the courtiers and the king laughed and slapped their knees. Lark wept.

In the next five days, more princes came and performed. A prince told shepherd jokes. His best joke was *Why is a bandit like a shepherd's staff?* The punch line was *They're both crooks.* The audience hooted with laughter. Lark rolled her eyes and wished for Robin. Then she wept.

A prince talked to his foot and pretended it was

"THE PRINCE JUGGLED CHEESES WHILE A
MOUSE STOOD ON HIS HEAD."

answering him. Lark recited under her breath, "Suffering, tribulation, death, drought, plague . . ." She wept.

After each performance she asked for permission to marry Robin, but the king always harrumphed no.

⚓ ⚓ ⚓

Two days remained before the wedding. Robin had heard nothing from Lark, and he was desperate to know what had happened. While he kneaded bread, he worried that the king had refused to let her marry him. He also feared she had decided his jokes weren't any good and had changed her mind about loving him.

Golly, standing at his elbow, talked about going to Ooth 'Town for their honeymoon to see the roundest clock in Biddle. Then she left to try on her wedding dress.

Someone in the bakery said the word *princess*.

Robin's head shot up. He stopped kneading.

"What seems to be the princess's troublicament?" Nat asked the schoolteacher.

"She never stops crying. Give me six scones."

Oh, no! Robin tried not to shout. "Why is she crying?"

"I'm not sure, but the king is going to marry her off to the first person who makes her laugh." The schoolteacher didn't know the person had to be a prince. "The contest is being held in the tournament arena."

Robin knocked over the kneading table and rushed out of the bakery. He had to think.

Back inside, Matt said, "The lad is flipliddified and madaddlated."

Robin paced up and down in the bakery yard. When the schoolteacher had said that Lark was weeping, Robin had thought it meant the king had refused to let them marry. And then, for one glorious moment, when the schoolteacher had described the contest, he'd thought it was for him, that it was Lark's way of bringing them together. But if it was, then why was she crying?

Something terrible must have happened.

He started striding to the castle. He'd tell the guards he wanted to compete in the contest, so they'd let him in. He had to find out what was going on, although he wouldn't be able to compete. He was much too upset to make up jokes.

But the Royal Drawbridge Guard wouldn't let him pass. The guard didn't even let him say what he was there for.

Robin was beside himself. He'd have to marry Golly, or he'd have to run away, far from Lark. Either way, he'd lose his love. On his way home, he broke down and cried.

Golly thought a weeping Robin was the funniest thing she'd ever seen. Jake gave her towels to dry off the dough as Robin kneaded it. She wiped and laughed for an hour or two. Then she went back to the Sleep In, to monogram an extra dozen handkerchiefs for her trousseau.

Through his tears Robin watched her go. He wished Golly were a princess and that Lark were an innkeeper's daughter. He wished the guard had let him in. He wished Lark were here right this second. He wished.

Nine

Late that night the fairy Ethelinda flew over Biddle. She'd been flying for seven years, ever since she'd left the court of Anura, the fairy queen. Anura had scolded her for not giving a single reward or punishment to a human in centuries. Ethelinda had explained that she was afraid to because she'd bungled it the last time.

"Conquer your fear!" Anura had commanded. "Mingle with humans. Reward and punish. Do not disobey me!"

Ethelinda hadn't obeyed, but she hadn't disobeyed either. She'd just stayed in the air. But now she had to land. Seven years of flying were too much, even for a fairy. She was exhausted. She looked for a secluded spot where humans were unlikely to come. Ah. There.

She landed in a clearing in Snoakes Forest and

stretched out under a pine tree, where she fell fast asleep.

The next morning, Jake packed a breakfast for Nat and sent him off early to chop wood. There was a lot to do today, and he wanted his two smart sons there to help him. He had to bake the usual quantities of bread, muffins, and scones, and he had to make the wedding cake for tomorrow.

Nat entered Snoakes Forest and went straight to the clearing where Ethelinda lay sleeping.

His footsteps woke her. She jumped up and took the shape of an old woman. She hoped whoever was coming wouldn't do anything that required a reward or a punishment.

Nat entered the clearing. Ethelinda frowned at his basket, hoping he didn't have food in there. "Good day," she said in a voice that wavered.

"Good day." Nat smiled and bowed. He opened the basket and took out a jug of blackberry juice, three hard-boiled partridge eggs, and two fig-and-almond scones.

The dreaded meal! Ethelinda thought. The fairy rules were very clear. She had to ask the human to share. If he did share, she had to reward him. If he did not, she had to punish him.

"Kind sir," she said, "would you share your victuals with me?"

Nat knew Jake's rule. "No, Mistress. I am enormvastically sorry, but our family doesn't give our edibles or sippables to anyone."

She had to punish him! "So be it," she said. So be what? What should she do? She was shaking like a leaf.

Nat ate his breakfast.

Ethelinda thought of making him choke on a bone. But eggs and scones don't have bones. She didn't want to make snakes and insects come out of his mouth, because that hadn't been a great success the last time.

Nat patted his mouth with his napkin and stood up. "Please excusition me. Time to get to work." He picked up his ax and went to an oak tree.

She got it! She waved her wand, which was invisible because of her disguise.

Nat swung the ax. It slammed into the air six inches from the tree and stopped. It wouldn't go an inch closer no matter how hard he pushed.

"Huh? What—" He swung again. The ax stopped again.

He examined the ax. The blade was as sharpcuttable as ever. Something was protecting the tree. He reached out, expecting the something to stop his hand. But nothing did. He swung again. The ax slammed into the air and stopped again.

He frowned at the old lady. Did she cause this?

But she was leaning back against an elm tree with her eyes closed. Besides, what could she have done?

It must have been that tree. He went to a pine tree and swung the ax. It stopped six inches from the bark.

He ran from tree to tree, trying to chop down one after another. But he couldn't, not a single one. He screamed, not an invented word, not a word at all, only a scream. He ran out of the clearing, still screaming.

Ethelinda resumed her fairy shape. She'd done it. Anura should be satisfied. Ethelinda flapped her wings—and barely got off the ground. She was still exhausted. She landed in a heap and stayed there.

When Nat got home from the forest, he was muttering to himself and swinging the ax wildly. Matt feared that he might have become as goofdoltish as Robin, and Jake agreed. They pinned Nat to the ground and took the ax.

Robin didn't notice. Tomorrow was the wedding. It would be the end of everything.

Matt packed a brunch. If Nat couldn't cut down a tree, he, Matt, certainly would be able to. Hadn't he been axchopperizing trees since he was seven years old? He set off while Jake mixed batter for three dozen muffin tins.

As soon as Ethelinda heard Matt coming, she turned herself back into the old lady. When he too refused to share his meal, she punished him exactly as she'd punished Nat.

Jake became seriously worried when Matt returned in the same state as Nat. Jake thought,

Now all my sons have lost their wits,
And Nat and Matt are having conniptions.

Jake couldn't go to the forest himself. He had twenty-seven loaves of bread in the oven plus all those muffins and no sane son to watch them. Robin would have to go. Jake packed a lunch and put the ax in

Robin's hand. He watched Robin go and then got to work on the wedding cake.

Ethelinda was delighted to see Robin. This punishment was terrific. She couldn't wait to use it again.

Robin put down his basket. It didn't occur to him to eat. He wasn't thinking at all. His mind was just bleating *Lark! Lark!* again and again. He staggered to a maple tree and raised his ax.

"Wait, kind sir!" Ethelinda went to him and stopped his hand. "Don't you want your lunch?"

What was she saying? Something about his lunch? He mumbled, "Don't want it."

"Oh, kind sir, may I have some?"

Lark! Lark! He raised the ax again.

"Kind sir!" Ethelinda shrieked. She grabbed the ax and wrestled it away from Robin. She faced him, panting. "May I eat some of your lunch?"

Lark! Lark! "Go ahead."

Go ahead?

Oh no! She handed the ax back to him. Now she had to reward him, which was where she'd made her biggest mistake the last time.

She opened his basket and took out a wedge of

Snetter cheese and a poppy-seed roll. What could she give him? She couldn't think of a single foolproof reward.

Robin began to chop down the maple.

Then Ethelinda remembered a reward the fairy queen, Anura, had told her about. It was a bit odd, but Anura said she'd used it hundreds of times and it had always worked.

Robin raised the ax again. One more chop and the maple would go over.

Ethelinda raised her invisible wand.

Robin swung the ax.

Ethelinda waved the wand.

The tree went over.

Honk! A golden goose stood on the stump, ruffling her golden feathers.

"HONK!"

Ten

Robin didn't notice the goose. He began to hack off the maple's branches.

"Oh," Ethelinda said, "what a beautiful golden goose!"

Robin felt a stab of exasperation. "You can have her."

Ethelinda stared in shock at him. And saw how unhappy he looked. "Why, what's the trouble, kind sir?"

He shook his head and chopped the maple into logs.

She made her voice sympathetic and comforting. "You can tell me. I'll understand."

The sweetness of her voice reached him. He looked up. Ethelinda made her expression kindly and patient.

He found himself talking. "I love Princess Lark

and I hate . . ." He told the whole story. It was a
relief to tell someone.

Ethelinda wasn't sure what good the goose would
do, but she had faith in Anura. "Pick up the
goose," she said. "Take her to the castle."

"I won't be able to get past the guards." He didn't
move.

"*Pick up the goose!*" Ethelinda bellowed.

He began to pick up the logs.

"With that goose, no one will stop you." Ethelinda
didn't know if this was true, but she'd make it true.

He dropped the logs and picked up the goose.

Honk!

He didn't believe no one would stop him, but he'd
try anyway.

Ethelinda asked where he was going, just to
make sure.

"To the princess."

At last. "The goose is sticky, so you may need these
words: *Loose, goose.* Don't forget them."

The goose was sticky? What did that mean? Robin
picked up a fallen leaf and touched it to the goose's
feathers. It stuck. He said, "Loose, goose." The leaf

fluttered to the ground.

Hmm. He had an idea. He left the clearing, walking fast.

Ethelinda brushed grass off her skirts. She felt rested, refreshed. She hurried after Robin. "I'll come too, kind sir. I may be able to help if anything goes wrong."

When he got near the Sleep In, Robin slowed to a saunter. If Golly didn't see him, he'd bang on the door. If he had to, he'd shove the goose up against her.

Upstairs in the inn, Golly was embroidering and looking out the window. Huh! she thought. There was Robin, with a goose in his arms and an old woman at his side. Golly squinted. What a fine golden goose. She frowned. Why wasn't he bringing the goose to her?

Because he was her dim-witted dearie. She laughed. "Look!"

Holly and Molly came to the window.

"We could cook the goose and share the feathers," Golly said.

The three of them ran downstairs and crowded out of the inn. Robin pretended not to see them and hurried off again.

"Dearie," Golly called, laughing. "Wait for me."

He kept going. They ran after him. Golly reached him first. She grabbed the goose's tail and pulled.

Honk!

Golly laughed. "Dearie!"

Robin heard her, but he didn't turn around. He hoped Holly and Molly would touch the goose too, and he hoped they'd stick too. Otherwise Golly had better look very funny, because she was all he'd have to make Lark laugh.

The goose pecked Golly's arm.

Yow! Golly tried to let go, but she couldn't. She stopped laughing. She was beginning to be annoyed.

Molly had almost reached the goose.

Golly yelled, "Don't touch the—"

"What?" Molly grasped Golly's elbow and didn't touch the goose.

"I'm stuck. Pull me off."

Molly pulled.

Honk!

But Golly stayed stuck.

"Help me, Holly!" Molly called, and held out her hand. "Pull!"

Holly took the hand and pulled.

Honk!

But Golly stayed stuck.

The three of them trotted after the goose. In a few minutes, Molly got tired. "I'm going home." She tried to let go of Golly's elbow. She yanked and tugged.

Honk!

She was stuck.

Holly tried to let go of Molly's hand, but she was stuck too.

Eleven

Hmm . . . Robin thought, glancing back. Whoever touches the goose becomes sticky. And the next person and the next become sticky too! He wondered how long a chain he could make. They did look funny, the three of them.

Golly was angry. "Dearie, stop this instant!"

Ethelinda didn't care a bit for Golly. Now *there* was a human who could use punishing.

Robin saw a mule and wagon in the distance, coming back from Biddle Castle

It was the Snettering-on-Snoakes chandler. He wondered where Robin was going with that goose and why Golly, Holly, and Molly were traipsing after him. And who was the old lady?

"Whoa, Jenny," he called to his mule.

Holly, Molly, and Golly yelled to the chandler to

set them loose. When he understood what they wanted, he tied a rope to Jenny's harness and threw the rope over Holly.

Oh, no! Robin thought. The goose can't be stronger than a mule.

"Pull, Jenny. Pull."

Jenny tried, but she couldn't. She got pulled instead.

The goose *is* stronger! Robin thought.

The chandler tried to jump down from his cart to see what was wrong, but he couldn't. He was stuck to his bench.

Robin glanced back and almost laughed. The beginning of a joke came to him. Why does a king always seem glum? But he was still too upset to think of the punch line.

The chandler and his cart and mule followed Robin and the golden goose. Holly and Molly kept hollering that Jenny should try harder. Golly kept screaming at Robin to stop, to listen, to behave himself . . . dearie.

The Royal Drawbridge Guard saw a strange parade, heading for Biddle Castle. He frowned. There was the chandler. But the chandler had left only a little while ago. Who were the others with him?

The chandler looked flustered. Could be trouble. The guard got his pike ready.

They came closer. The guard wondered why the chandler and his mule and wagon and three wenches were following a lad with a golden goose. Why were the wenches shouting? Why did the mule look so confused? And who was the old lady?

Then the guard understood. The lad was really a prince! A contestant! The guard started laughing and put down his pike. This was so funny. It was sure to win. He bowed as Robin approached

Robin thought, He's letting me in! The old lady is right! Maybe he'd like to come along too. He called, "Help yourself to a feather."

The guard lunged at the goose.

Honk!

The guard was stuck.

Robin was going by the Royal Kitchen Door just as the Royal Third Assistant Cook stepped outside.

My, the cook thought, that's a fine pair of goose feet, perfect for pickling. He reached out and grabbed the goose's right foot.

Honk!

⚓ ⚓ ⚓

In the Royal Tournament Arena Lark wept on. So far seventy-five princes had tried to make her laugh. The king and the Royal Nobles were merrier than ever before. But Lark's eyes hurt from crying so much. Two Royal Laundresses worked day and night to keep her in fresh hankies.

Right now a prince was saying "Fiffifferall" over and over. At first no one had laughed, but after a few minutes a Royal Baroness had begun to giggle, and then the Royal Chief Councillor had joined in, and soon everyone was laughing heartily.

Except Lark, of course.

A commotion at the arena's entrance drowned out the prince. Heads turned. Lark didn't look up.

Robin, Holly, Molly, Golly, the Royal Drawbridge Guard, and the Royal Third Assistant Cook jogged into the arena. Behind them, the chandler, Jenny, and the cart clattered along. Ethelinda skipped and leaped and waved her arms in the air, to add to the silliness.

Robin saw Lark. There she was. Weeping! Her sweet face was unutterably sad. She was wiping her eyes and staring at her lap. She hadn't even seen him.

He broke into a run. *Lark! Oh, Lark!*

Twelve

King Harrumphrey and the courtiers saw the goose parade and roared with laughter. Even the prince saying "Fiffifferall" laughed. The Earl of Pildenue fell out of his seat, laughing. Dame Cloris woke up and started laughing. King Harrumphrey rocked back and forth on his throne.

Lark wept and never looked up. Where was her love now? Did he miss her?

Robin moaned. Whatever had happened to Lark must have been—must still be—awful. He began to cry in sympathy.

Under the laughter and the shrieks, Lark heard a new sound. She closed her eyes to hear better. Someone else was weeping.

Robin ran across the arena. He shouted, "Oh, Lark! Oh, my love! Oh, don't cry!"

She opened her eyes. Robin? Here? Yes! She smiled

rapturously at him. Just at him—because she didn't notice the guard, the cook, Ethelinda, Golly, Molly, Holly, the chandler, Jenny, the cart, or the goose.

She's smiling! Robin thought. He smiled back at her through his tears.

Lark jumped up, knocking over her outdoor throne. Then she saw the spectacle behind Robin. They were so funny! She ran down the arena steps, laughing as she ran.

Ethelinda laughed too. Giving a successful reward was its own reward.

Robin thought of the punch line for the joke about why a king seems glum. He laughed. His laughter shook the goose.

Honk!

Golly shrieked, "Dearie! Get away from that princess."

Robin said, "Loose, goose."

Holly, Molly, Golly, the chandler, the mule, the cart, the Royal Drawbridge Guard, and the Royal Third Assistant Cook were released from their hold on the goose and each other.

Royal Nobles poured onto the field. They surrounded Robin and bowed to him and shouted,

"Congratulations!" Ethelinda stood at the edge of the crowd. She was sure she'd never have trouble with rewards again, now that she'd found the goose.

"Harrumph."

The crowd parted for King Harrumphrey.

He was delighted to see Larkie laughing again. And this young prince had done it cleverly. Dressing like a commoner—very smart. He'd make a fine son-in-law. "We are pleased to make your harrumphance, Your Highness." He put his arm around Robin's shoulder. "What kingdom do you harrumph from?"

Highness? Kingdom? Who did the king think he was? Robin knelt. "I live in Snettering-on-Snoakes, Sire. I'm Robin, the baker's son."

He *is* a commoner! the king thought. He's that blasted baker's son.

"I want to marry him," Lark said.

King Harrumphrey wanted to throw him into the Royal Dungeon. But he couldn't, not with Larkie smiling at the boy in that demented way.

Golly opened her mouth to say that she was marrying Robin.

"Son," the king said, "only a prince could win the harrumph."

Golly shut her mouth.

Robin thought, So that's why Lark was weeping. He thought of weeping again himself, but he couldn't stop smiling at her.

King Harrumphrey turned to his daughter. "You don't want to harrumphy him, honeyharrumph. We'll give him a harrumphdred golden coins instead."

Ethelinda was furious. She hated a snob. Couldn't the king tell what a fine lad Robin was?

"No, Father. He doesn't want a gift."

"A harrumphdred golden coins and a golden cage for that golden harrumph."

"No thank you, Your Majesty."

"Father, I'm going to cry again."

"Don't harrumph. We hate it when you harrumph. Let us think." He couldn't let her marry a commoner. What would his Royal Forebears have done? Well, King Humphrey IV would have devised a test. What kind of test? Hmm . . .

"We will consent to the harrumphage," he said, "if the lad can pass three harrumphs. For the first harrumph he must find someone who can drink a whole cellar full of harrumph." He saw Lark's expression.

"Very fine harrumph. Only the best."

Golly laughed. Her dearie would never pass the test.

Who could drink so much? Robin wondered. And what's harrumph? Beet juice? Bat's milk?

I can do it, Ethelinda thought. I can drink anything.

"The second harrumph is to find someone who can eat a hill of harrumphs as tall as our Royal Glass Hill."

Now what's harrumph? Robin thought. Skunk sausages?

"And the third harrumph . . ." The king paused for effect " . . is to come to Biddle Castle on a ship that harrumphs on land or water."

Lark frowned. "What?"

"A harrumph that sails on land or harrumph." No commoner can pass these tests, King Harrumphrey thought. But if this upstart does, we'll dream up three more tests, and then three more. As many as it takes.

Thirteen

The third test might be hard, Ethelinda thought.

Robin couldn't imagine how he'd pass any of them. He was going to lose Lark all over again.

"The tests are impossible," Lark wailed.

"Sweetie, this harrumph has already made you laugh, and you and we thought that was imharrumphible."

But that was because he's my love, she thought. And because he's funnier than anyone else.

Robin remembered that the old lady had said she might be able to help him some more. He turned her way, and she winked at him—although she still wasn't sure about the last test.

Robin began to have a suspicion about her. "I'll try," he told the king. He bowed. "Farewell." Farewell, my love.

"Farewell." Lark smiled bravely.

Robin picked up the goose and started out of the arena. Ethelinda walked at his side. Golly began to go with them, but the fairy waved her invisible wand.

Golly's feet wouldn't move, no matter how hard she tried. "Dearie, I want to come with you."

He kept walking.

"Get back here and help me, dearie."

He walked faster.

When they were out of sight of the castle, Robin said, "You're a fairy, aren't you?"

Smart human! Ethelinda resumed her normal form. *Honk!*

Robin staggered back. She was gigantic! And those wings! Pink, fleshy, and vast.

He thought it might be a good idea to bow, so he did. "Will you help me?"

She turned herself into a hungry-and-thirsty-looking beggar. "This is the right shape for the first two tests, don't you think?"

He nodded. They waited a half hour so it would seem as if he had spent some time searching for someone. Then they started back to the tournament arena.

Meanwhile, King Harrumphrey was annoyed because he'd used up seven hundred kegs of cider flooding the basement of the Royal Museum of Quest Souvenirs. Worse, he had no idea how he was going to un-flood it when Robin's person failed to drink it dry.

But in case whoever it was succeeded, the king had ordered the Royal Kitchen to cook thousands of meatballs for the second test. Most likely everybody at the castle was going to be eating meatballs till meatballs came out of their eyeballs.

Lark felt a little hope when she saw the beggar, who was as skinny as one of the goose's legs. His cracked and chapped tongue hung out, for certain the driest tongue in Biddle. King Harrumphrey started to worry.

Holly, Molly, the chandler, the guard, and the cook had left. Golly had stayed, although the spell on her feet had worn off.

At the museum a Royal Servant opened the trapdoor to the cellar. Cider lapped against the ceiling. Robin put the goose down and stood next to Lark to watch.

Ethelinda used her fairy powers to discover if anything was in the cellar besides cider. Seventeen rats, drinking and swimming. She made them vanish. She didn't want their whiskers anywhere near her

"TILL MEATBALLS CAME OUT OF THEIR
EYEBALLS."

mouth, and she didn't want King Harrumphrey to claim that she'd had help drinking a single sip.

The servant handed her a ladle.

A ladle! It would take years with a ladle. Ethelinda waved it aside and lowered her head into the cellar.

She began to drink. The first seventy gallons were delicious, but after that she wished someone had thought to add cinnamon. When a hundred kegs were gone, she could no longer reach low enough to drink. The servant went for a ladder.

While they waited, Ethelinda said, "Thank you, Sire. I would have perished of thirst if not for you. I only hope there's enough here to satisfy me."

King Harrumphrey nodded and tried to look gracious. Lark and Robin held hands while he whispered jokes into her ear. Her favorite was Why are elves delicious? She thought the answer was hysterical: Because they're brownies.

Golly glared at Lark, Robin, the goose, and the beggar. She swore to give that beggar a kick if he ever showed up at her inn.

The king thought up two additional tests, in case he needed them. He'd make Robin find someone who could play twenty musical instruments at once and someone who could go up the Royal Grand Staircase on his head.

The servant returned with a ladder. Ethelinda descended two rungs and drank.

In an hour the cellar was dry. King Harrumphrey inspected it carefully, hoping against hope that he'd find at least a drop of cider, but he didn't.

It took Ethelinda one and a half hours to finish the meatballs. When she was done, she bowed to the king and burped.

King Harrumphrey said, "Robin, you must harrumph back here in two hours with a harrumph that can sail on land or sea."

Lark said, "You didn't say there was a time limit."

"Two harrumphs and no longer. By Royal Harrumph!"

Fourteen

In a field beyond the castle, Robin patted the goose and waited for Ethelinda to create the ship. Instead, she sat on the ground and put her head in her hands.

He cleared his throat uneasily. "Is there a problem?"

"I'm thinking." She could make a beautiful ship, one that could weather any storm. But on shore it wouldn't budge. She could make a wonderful carriage that would go anywhere on land, even without a road. But in water it would sink.

Robin said, "What if the sails turn into wings when the boat reaches the shore?"

"Then the king would say it's a bird on land and not a boat."

The minutes ticked by. An hour passed. The sky began to get dark.

An hour and a half passed. The stars came out.

Maybe the lad was on the right track with the wings idea, Ethelinda thought.

Fifteen more minutes passed.

What if she filled the hold with wings? Not birds, just wings. When the ship was on land, the wings would fly up against the ceiling of the hold and lift the ship off the ground.

That was the way to do it. She waved her wand.

Robin gasped. The boat was beautiful, painted yellow with blue trim. The sails were blindingly white. If it could move on land, it would pass the test.

But King Harrumphrey probably still wouldn't let him marry Lark. The king would think of more and more tests, until the fairy got sick of tests and left him.

I have to think of a way to make this the last one, Robin thought. He stared at the ship. It needed something, something to show what kind of ship it was. It needed a pennant.

A pennant! That was it.

"Is there any empty land far from here where I could be prince?" he asked.

Ethelinda thought for a moment. "You could be

Prince of the Briny Isles. This ship will get you there in seven years. You'll starve to death, though, unless you like anchovies."

"That doesn't matter." If he actually had to go there, his idea would have failed. "Would you make a pennant that says 'Prince Robin of the Briny Isles'?"

She did, and she dressed him as a prince, in a red satin robe and a doublet with diamond buttons. On his head she placed a silver crown set with rubies.

They mounted a plank onto the ship. It set sail across the field. The boat was a glorious sight, skimming a foot above the ground, its sails bellying out in the breeze.

When the boat reached the castle, it descended into the moat, to prove that it could sail on water too. Then it rose again and stopped a few yards from Lark, the king, and Golly, who were standing near the castle drawbridge. Ethelinda, disguised as a nobleman, threw a ladder over the side. Robin and the nobleman climbed down and bowed. The goose remained on deck, strutting up and down and honking.

Lark curtsied and said, "Your Highness."

King Harrumphrey scowled. The lad looked better,

but a baker's son in prince's clothing was still a baker's son.

Golly gasped. Robin had passed every test. He was going to marry the princess! How dared he? She screamed, "Dearie, I wouldn't marry you if you were the stupidest lad in Biddle. You led me—"

"Be silent," Robin said. "I command it."

Golly was so surprised, she fell silent.

He sounds princely, King Harrumphrey thought, but still . . .

Ethelinda said, "I am the Duke of Halibutia and the envoy of the King of the Briny Isles. He sent me here to find an heir worthy to rule after his death, and I have found him. Prince Robin has more natural royalty than anyone I've ever encountered."

"Sire," Robin said, "I have passed your tests. Give me your daughter's hand in marriage."

"Do, Father. Please."

Robin continued. "Then we shall depart for my kingdom, which is seven years' sailing from here." He held his breath, hoping.

King Harrumphrey frowned. Since the envoy—a duke!—had chosen Robin, then the lad had truly become a prince. But seven years! Even if they turned around and came back as soon as they got there, the king still wouldn't see his Larkie for fourteen years.

He couldn't live for fourteen years without the sight of her. "Harrumph. Er, we admit that you are a prince, but can't you stay here? Can't those Briny Harrumphs do without you?"

"If I stay here, I'll just be a baker's son."

"Father . . ."

King Harrumphrey looked at his daughter. She was half smiling. He knew what would turn that smile into a laugh. And he knew what would turn it into a frown and tears.

There had been enough tears. "No, you will not be a baker's harrumph. You will be a Harrumph Prince of Biddle."

Lark and Robin hugged each other. They danced across the Royal Drawbridge and back again.

Robin was so happy, he decided to try out a joke on King Harrumphrey. He said, "Why does a king always seem glum?"

King Harrumphrey frowned. What was the fellow talking about?

Lark was thrilled. Now Father would see what

Robin was really like. "Why?" she said.

"Because he's . . ." Robin sighed dramatically. ". . . a sire."

The king stared. Then he got it. A sire. A sigh-er! He started laughing. "Har har harrumph." It was the funniest joke he'd ever heard. "A harrumph-er!" This commoner-turned-prince would liven up the castle. "Har harrumph har. Harrumph har har."

Lark preferred the yardstick-ruler joke. But if Father loved this one, that was all that mattered.

Epilogue

Jake was as opposed to the match between Robin and Lark as King Harrumphrey had been. He said,

> *"I forbid the marriage with Princess Lark.*
> *I would rather see the boy wed a barracuda."*

King Harrumphrey offered to elevate Jake to the rank of earl and to knight Nat and Matt, who had finally recovered from Ethelinda's spell.

The three of them refused to become nobles. However, Jake agreed to the wedding when the king named him Royal Chief Poet and named Nat and Matt Royal Co-Chief Dictionarians in charge of adding new words to Biddlish.

Robin and Lark were married within a week, and the whole population of Snettering-on-Snoakes was invited, even though every one of them was a commoner.

King Harrumphrey performed the wedding ceremony, although Lark and Robin weren't sure if the harrumphiage they were entering into was their marriage or their carriage.

Dame Cloris snored straight through the king's speech. Golly stayed awake. She sat next to the chandler and decided he was the man for her. If she couldn't boss him around, she'd boss Jenny the mule.

After the ceremony Robin told a joke:

"Why is a horse like a wedding?"

He waited, but not one of the guests could think of the answer, so he told them, "They both need a groom."

Lark laughed and laughed. She felt so proud of Robin, the funniest prince in Biddle history.

Jake wasn't sure he got the joke. His own Horsteed had never had a groom in his life. But he smiled and waited for the laughter to subside, so he could recite a poem to Robin.

"I thought to maiden Golly you'd be wed,
  But you married Princess Lark in place of her."

Robin and Lark thanked Ethelinda over and over for her help. Their gratitude went a long way toward restoring her confidence, and she was certain she'd never make another mistake.

The party after the ceremony was held on the bank of Snoakes Stream. Robin and Lark waded right in and pulled courtiers and commoners in after them for a Royal Splashfest. The golden goose waddled in too and splashed and honked at everybody. Lark was in heaven, splashing dukes and counts, and having them splash her right back.

And they all lived happily ever after.

Harrumph!

Honk!

The End.

Read the other hilarious Princess Tales!

Pb 0-06-051841-3

Before the fairy returned, she stirred up magical trouble in *The Fairy's Mistake*—just one of three delightfully funny fairy tales included in *The Princess Tales, Volume One*.

And meet Ella, a princess caught in a fairy's foolish spell...

Hc 0-06-027510-3
Pb 0-06-440705-5
Pb 0-06-055886-5 (rack)

Ella Enchanted is a charming Cinderella story, with princes, ogres, wicked stepsisters, and a fairy-tale ending fit for a princess. Now a movie from Miramax!

HarperTrophy®
An Imprint of HarperCollins*Publishers*
www.harperchildrens.com

AVON BOOKS
Also available from HarperChildren's Audio